"PERCEPTI ... E
PASSAGE FROM CHILDHOOD TO MANHOOD
. . . UPDIKE PROMISES TO REWARD US FOR
MANY YEARS TO COME."
—*The New York Times Book Review*

"LYRICAL . . . TIMELESS . . . Updike is one of the
few young writers to stylize in the old manner—lush,
rhythmic, in tune with the weather. His smooth prose
unfolds into elaborate pastoral motifs."
—*Boston Globe*

"Quiet but resonating tales that reflect a sensitivity to
character and place and an elegiac sense of the seasons
of life . . . the even tenor of the fifteen stories in this
impressive, well-crafted and often moving collection
conveys the almost imperceptible movement that
occurs in the passage from birth to young adulthood."
—*Publishers Weekly*

"This voice, along with the poignant juncture at which
the characters stand, gives the stories many luminous
moments and passages."
—*Village Voice*

DAVID UPDIKE teaches English in Cambridge,
Massachusetts. His stories have appeared in *The New
Yorker* and in the volume *Twenty Under Thirty*. He is
the author of a children's book, *A Winter's Tale*.

Out on the Marsh

Stories by
David Updike

A PLUME BOOK

NEW AMERICAN LIBRARY

A DIVISION OF PENGUIN BOOKS USA INC., NEW YORK
PUBLISHED IN CANADA BY
PENGUIN BOOKS CANADA LIMITED, MARKHAM, ONTARIO

NAL BOOKS ARE AVAILABLE AT QUANTITY DISCOUNTS WHEN USED TO
PROMOTE PRODUCTS OR SERVICES. FOR INFORMATION PLEASE WRITE
TO PREMIUM MARKETING DIVISION, NEW AMERICAN LIBRARY,
1633 BROADWAY, NEW YORK, NEW YORK 10019.

Some of the stories included in this book
first appeared in *The New Yorker.*

PLUME TRADEMARK REG. U.S. PAT. OFF. AND FOREIGN COUNTRIES
REGISTERED TRADEMARK—MARCA REGISTRADA
HECHO EN BRATTLEBORO, VT., U.S.A.

SIGNET, SIGNET CLASSIC, MENTOR, ONYX, PLUME, MERIDIAN
and NAL BOOKS are published *in the United States* by New American Library,
a division of Penguin Books USA Inc., 1633 Broadway,
New York, New York 10019, and *in Canada* by Penguin Books Canada Limited,
2801 John Street, Markham, Ontario L3R 1B4

First Plume Printing, May, 1989

1 2 3 4 5 6 7 8 9

PRINTED IN THE UNITED STATES OF AMERICA

Dedicated to my parents

Contents

Out on the Marsh

First Impressions

The Garden

Starting with our first, headlong splash into the world, our lives unfold as a series of expanding boundaries, like the swelling circles caused by a stone thrown into a placid pond. From the womb we graduate to our mother's arms, and then to the light, airy enclosure of our hospital room, to be held in orderly rows of cribs with our sullen, breathless peers. Days later, still blind and helpless, we are taken by taxi cab to a small dark room with flying elephants, lace curtains, and the hovering, luminous faces of admiring relatives parading past us like the planets of a newly discovered solar system. With time we learn to walk, to crawl, to run; to throw a stone, a stick, a ball, and from there to grope along toward the more difficult tasks of adulthood.

From a small room in New York City, I gathered my first impressions of the outside world: the muted bawl of

3

fire engines and police cars, the ebb and flow of night and day, the shifting shades and patterns of light thrown onto my ceiling by the beams of cars passing on the street below. My sister, aged two and perhaps confused by my sudden appearance in the world, introduced me to the laws of momentum, rolling me the length of the hall in my wheeled crib until I crashed with a dull, jarring thump into the wall at its far end.

Later in our new house in Massachusetts, I learned to crawl, slowly exploring the vast, white expanse of carpet, conducting tiny experiments on the nature of heat, my small, pale hands groping in the rhombic shapes of sunlight that fell through the window nearby. When I first sat outdoors, I took in the flight and twitter of birds as they drew mysterious criss-crossing lines across the foggy field of my vision and the blue translucent sky. I was hoisted into my father's arms and held above him on a single, outstretched hand, staring down at the surface of my world as my happiness slowly dissolved, and my laughter turned into a baited, breathless bawl.

Two years later we moved again, to the house where I would spend my childhood and from where I now receive my first pale signals of memory, the first lasting impressions made on my small and maleable mind: the smell of lilacs, the sound of rain, the mysterious emanation of heat rising from sun-warmed stones. On all fours I moved across the surface of the earth, examining artifacts of the natural world: a broken twig, a clump of earth, a dry and decomposing bee. Beside me iris leaves, like overlapping spears, swayed and trembled with translucent drops of dew.

Hot, sunny mornings often found me at the top of the

steps, staring across the surface of our scruffy lawn. On weak and wobbly legs I made my way down past the garden and along the brink of the stone wall to where the lawn extended itself in a peninsula of lush, verdant green. The grass was thick and wet with dew, and a wall of heart-shaped leaves rose up beside me, and clusters of lilacs hung down in purple bunches. I ambled toward them and with small, ungainly hands pressed their dewy petals to my face, lips, nose, eyes, forehead, inhaling less by smell than by osmosis—an experiment abruptly ending when I spat out the crushed and bitter flowers I had chewed.

Along one side of our lawn there was a small, unkempt garden filled with leaves and tall, swaying poppies, and a pumpkin that appeared each fall. It was there I first observed the goings on of nature, the overlapping lives of the few animals who made it their home: bees, butterflies, snakes, spiders, toads, mice, moles, and the birds who fluttered down from surrounding trees. One day, as I sat in the grass and watched, our cat slipped out through the back door, came up the steps and crouched by the edge of the garden, looking in, his tail slowly stirring the limpid air. In time, his own inactivity induced in a nearby bird a lapse of judgment or care, and there followed a few short stolen steps, a sudden, desperate leap, a tussle among the leaves until the cat reappeared, bearing its unlucky struggling captive between its slowly closing jaws.

As I got older, the lawn seemed to grow smaller—measured against the distance I could throw a stone, or the effort required to sprint across it—and I began to explore its remotest regions: the mossy canyon between our shed and the neighbor's garage; the grove of pine trees from which we could spy on our neighbor (an aging beauty sleeping in a sunlit chair); the various caves and tunnels formed by overgrown shrubs and bushes.

On summer nights, my sister and I sat out on the front steps, watching the endless stream of cars, and listening to the sweet, melancholy strains of that summer's hit that rose from the open roofs of passing convertibles. I began to commune with other children of the neighborhood and make excursions to other people's houses, and there, tucked into clean white sheets, I experienced the novel thrill of other mothers' good-night kisses.

In autumn, the spectrum of smells shifted to burning leaves and chestnuts, the colors to orange, russet, brown. I loved the way the garden looked with its wilting, broken stalks and fading flowers, and the pumpkin, alternately frozen by the moon and warmed by the sun, sinking into the tired earth. I loved the clouds of my own frozen breath, the lifeless branches of the trees, the silver moon arcing across a starless sky. And I loved the steady encroachment of winter, the diminishing gap between the end of school and the fall of night.

And then one evening my grandparents would appear on their annual visit, the headlights of their car shining across the yard like the eyes of a frightened cat. My brother and sister and I would sprint across the yard to greet them, arriving as the doors creaked open and my grandparents stiffly emerged, like messengers from the past. My grandfather, a looming, gentle giant in the half-light, smelling faintly of hay, would slowly start to laugh for no particular reason, his false teeth gleaming dully, and with the steady measured step of someone who had

6

already survived two heart attacks, he would move around to the trunk to unlock it and reveal the tins of pretzels and bags of apples he had brought 300 miles.

Later a younger brother and sister were born, confusing the simplicity of my world. On my seventh birthday I was given a small dog which, when she mysteriously died a month or two later, gave me my first vague inklings of eternity, tears streaming down my stinging, breathless cheeks. Spring came, and I felt the wonderful solidity of bare earth—dirt released from ice and melting snow, the reassuring crunch of sand beneath my running, stomping feet. The air was soft, the sun warm, the earth moist and firm. In the backyard the dead yellow grass yielded to tufts of deep, bright green, and from the lifeless thicket of the garden sprouted a hopeful, purple blur of crocuses. The forsythia bush which, a month before, had served in my artic world as an igloo, now bloomed into a florid, yellow hill. Birds tugged worms from the softened soil, grass grew, and one Sunday morning my sister and I, dressed in our best clothes, paraded through the undergrowth with small wicker baskets, collecting Easter eggs our parents had hidden the night before. A month later the smell of lilacs filled my favorite peninsula of yard and I made expeditions there, re-creating my own, private ritual of spring, pressing the dewy flowers to my face, absorbing their fragrance with all available senses which, even then, had come to include a sense of passing time.

The slow evolutions of the seasons brought me on a rising spiral through my childhood and, when I was about ten or so, from the house where I had grown up to another house, surrounded by woods and fields and marsh—a broader, more elemental world I welcomed.

We moved in spring, but it was not until the following fall that my grandmother, visiting us for the first time alone (my grandfather having died the previous spring), asked my father to drive her over to the old house to "say good-bye." I did not understand the nature of our mission but, sensing my father's reluctance and his need of moral support, I went along.

By the time we got there it was almost dark. The new people had already moved in and we drove around back, parked on the street, and walked up the rough stones of the driveway to stand by the white picket fence at the edge of the backyard, looking into this place where, somehow, we no longer belonged. Everything seemed strangely simple, rustic, and already smaller than I remembered it: the delapidated shed, the unkempt garden, the bent and aging elm, the patches of packed earth we had worn smooth in summer kickball games that were already beginning to grow over in the absence of children. As we stood in silence the darkness settled around us like snow, and a familiar dog bark rose up in the thin air and fell away. When it seemed enough time had passed I looked up at my grandmother, surprised by the streams of tears that had formed in the furrows of her cheeks, the strange worried look that had come into her eyes. My father fidgeted, my grandmother sighed, and as if that was our cue we all turned and walked back down the driveway in our small, somber procession, my father leading the way, anxious to be gone, as if to protect his son from what his mother had revealed.

Sounds
and Shadows

When I was six I went off to school, leaving the safety of my house and backyard. On the first day I walked the several blocks there with my mother, but later with my sister, and then with Mathew Barrows, a tall, thin, hard-kneed boy with whom I soon became friends. He lived in an old red house near ours, and we would play together, crawling through the bushes in our yards, scaling the mossy canyon between our shed and the neighbor's barn, and with little toy soldiers playing army in the dirt.

A few hundred yards to the right lived another friend, Ned Vine, in the big white house that served as rectory for the Episcopal Church where his father was minister. It was in front of his house that, as a boy of four or five, I had fled in tears from an overaffectionate "bear" who had tried to embrace me during a fourth of July parade. And it was Ned Vine who had once told me that his dog Rusty chased cars because he was irritated by the sight of his own reflection in their shiny hubcaps—a theory that, even then, seemed to me unlikely.

Our houses were connected by a ribbon of sidewalk that lay between them, and I knew every inch of its varied surface—squares of pale pavement, stretches of rough dirt and scattered stones, places where the smooth, packed earth was criss-crossed by gnarled roots, worn smooth and white like bones. On this sidewalk I had learned to walk, to run, to ride a bike, and it was there one afternoon, that Ned and I found ourselves on opposite sides of a roadblock lorded over by two neighborhood bullies. One was rather plump, with a round face and horn-rimmed glasses, and the other was thin and small with an amused smirk of defiance on his hard, white face. Neither Ned nor I were fighting types and, as they refused to let us pass, we retreated to our respective houses, recommunicated by telephone, and made other arrangements to meet. I took the long way around to his house, and we spent the afternoon together, but later, when I returned home, it was with a distinct sense of trepidation. And though the two boys were gone, the red wheelbarrow with which they had blocked our path was still there, emitting a palpable scent of evil.

But the worlds of children are small, and as there lay only a few hundred yards between my house and that of the smaller of these two boys, we soon became friends, against all my instincts and inclinations. Children's lives operate by their own unspoken rules beyond the realm of adults and, once befriended, there was no way to escape. To have asked for my parents' intervention would have only furthered the case against me, and it was Billy Purse, and not them, to whom I would eventually have had to answer.

He was small for his age, had a thin, hard face touched with freckles and ears that stuck out somewhat farther than he would have liked. A shock of brown hair, carefully preserved and clipped at a jaunty angle by the barber, fell across his forehead, and he was in the habit of keeping it back from his eyes with an impudent flick of his head—a gesture that, in our private code, signaled a certain brand of toughness. He was fond of describing things as "sharp," a catch-all term of admiration for bikes and cars and older girls. His house was old and tired and gave off an aura of subdued poverty: the lamp shades were yellow and the floors were covered with a faded, cracked linoleum. His mother was a lean, sullen woman with graying hair and a drawn, unhappy face, like the waitresses in urban luncheonettes. Billy had two brothers, one older and one younger, and he alternated between beating up one and being beaten up by the other; now and then they were all three beaten up by their father, a bearish man who sometimes drank too much.

Though small for his age Billy was two years older than I and thus, in the popular vocabulary of the time, he was able to "take me," that is, out-wrestle me, and otherwise lord over me in the comforting knowledge of physical superiority. What he did to frighten me I can only faintly remember. He inflicted less physical pain than fear, and held me under the constant threat of humiliation. One hot summer day I was alone in the house, enjoying his absence, happily watching a children's show on television. At one point our host, an affable robot named Clank, invited the children in the audience, and those of us at home, to dance to the jaunty twist music played by a troupe of musical baboons. For the first time in my life I felt the impulse to join in and, having checked the other rooms to make sure I was alone I returned and began to dance, feeling both happy and foolish. I was just beginning to enjoy myself when I sensed someone nearby and looked in the doorway. There, staring up at me from the floor, was the insipid, smiling face of Billy Purse, who had somehow slithered into the house unheard. He immediately fell into paroxysms of laughter, writhing on the floor like a serpent. I almost started to cry at the cruelty of it all, and begged him, pleaded with him to stop, all the while knowing that it was too late, that the fatal mistake had been made, that I was destined to spend the rest of the day, or week, or month, in the unhappy shadow of his derision.

Among his other talents was that of driving my real friends away, and so I was not only trapped by him but denied the company of those who might have saved me. Billy and I attended different schools, and thus our shared world was that of the neighborhood—sidewalks, streets, backyards, the woods that lay, like a vast, unexplored domain of evil, on the hill behind our houses. Our relationship thrived in a world of shadows, beyond the reach of other children and adults. In the damp space between the Pickards' barn and a cool stone wall, in the scented darkness of "slippery pines," we sat on a decaying log, Billy smoking a cigarette and forcing me to do the same. We roamed as far as "second sands," a sinister place frequented by tough older boys and the straw-haired blondes they brought on the backs of their motor cycles, and Baker's pond, a murky oval of water rimmed with mud and weeds and sleepy, green-eyed frogs. Hot summer days were often spent down at the town wharf—I, vaguely plotting my escape, Billy bouncing the minnows he had caught off the dock, watching their stunned attempts at recovery as they flickered grotesquely, stirring the waters beneath his feet.

Our relationship reached its acutest pitch at dusk, in those precious, waning minutes before Billy was called home, and I was finally allowed to return to mine. Late one autumn afternoon, as darkness began to sift down through the trees like smoke, and the barks of neighboring dogs rose in a strange and melancholy chorus, Billy and I were playing football in the backyard, "one on one." I had the misfortune of hitting his nose with my elbow and found myself backing away from him, trying to explain that it was an accident. "I didn't mean it," I pleaded, looking back at his hard, pale eyes, at the strange, satisfied look that had come into his face. "It was an accident," I repeated, and then felt the tight grip of his hands on my wrists, his leg behind me, then the painful thump of the earth as I hit the ground.

"No it wasn't," Billy said. "Now take it back." And then he was on top of me, his knees pressed against the soft flesh of my upper arms, his face looming above me like a demon.

"It was an accident," I inanely repeated, staring up at his thin lips from which a tremulous glob of spit was preparing to fall.

He was not allowed out after dark, and so I came to love the coming of winter, the diminishing gap between the end of school and the fall of night. Neither was he allowed out if it rained, and so I silently willed its coming, cheered on the gathering clouds and lowering sky, loving the very sound of thunder, of rain on the roof, the splash of puddles, signaling my freedom for another day.

Perhaps it was because Billy was poor, my mother socially conscious, that she was forever botching schemes I had carefully contrived to avoid him—inviting him to the beach with us, or to Fourth of July fireworks—an event I had looked forward to for months because he would not be there. On those hot summer days I seemed to have a perpetual headache, and these became the origin of other, nonexistent headaches I would report to my parents so I would not have to go to school—not because I hated school, but so that, when it was over, I would not have to see Billy Purse. And on those happy days at home I dreaded the inevitable hour when school ended, for it was then that Billy would be arriving at my house, wondering if I could "come out." As the hour approached I retreated to my room, closed the door, crawled in under the covers, and tried to will myself to sleep, hating the very sound of the doorbell when it rang, the thin strains of Billy's voice that found their way upstairs, poisoning my solitude. It was only with the front door closing that I felt free at last, released from the chance of his company.

My parents were having their own problems at this time, and it was perhaps natural that they should see my troubles as a consequence of theirs. A few years before, I had walked in on one of their fights and when I asked what was wrong I was told "Daddy wants to leave us and marry Mrs. Schroon, that's what!" and the plate my mother was holding then dropped to the floor and shattered, pieces of ceramic blue sliding across the linoleum like fragments of an exploded star.

But for whatever reasons, my parents knew I was unhappy, and that my headaches, whether real or otherwise, were symptomatic of something else, and so they decided to take me to a child psychologist in the city.

Mrs. Randall was a pleasant, middle-aged woman with gray hair and a big old dog who used to lie around on the floor and sleep while we talked. Her office was warm and sunny and filled with toys designed, it seemed, for children much younger than I—building blocks and dolls and model cars, a plastic air rifle which, when its two ends were compressed, shot Ping-Pong balls with surprising velocity. I spent my time building elaborate castles with these wooden blocks, peopling them with small dolls and then, toward the end of my "session," demolishing them with well-placed shots from the gun.

Although I do not remember once mentioning Billy Purse, I enjoyed going to see her for other, subtler reasons—getting out of school early, escaping town while my friends were still trapped in their classrooms, sitting in the warm, cozy office while Mrs. Randall quietly asked me questions. I spent much of my time on the floor, brushing the sleeping dog whose only activity, in a day filled with the unwanted attentions of unhappy children, was to occasionally stand up and reposition himself in the shifting squares of sunlight that fell through the window. Now and then Mrs. Randall and I stirred him to consciousness, put on his leash, and took him for a short walk outside. And while we stood together in the soft, warm sunlight and Bruno sniffed around on the sun-warmed earth and unceremoniously relieved himself on a nearby tree, it seemed to me that Bruno and Mrs. Randall and I were playing some pleasant, elaborate trick on the world.

In the summer, my parents took us to a small island off the coast of Maine, and later I arranged to spend a week with Ned Vine and his family in New Hampshire. When I returned in the fall I was amazed to discover that Billy no longer sought me out with the same regularity, that he had shifted his attentions to Jim Cook in whom, when I saw them together on the street, I detected the same sense of terror I had once felt in myself. My view of the world was further modified when, a few months later, I learned that Billy and Jim Cook had finally come to blows, and that Jim had bloodied Billy's nose. After that he seemed to spend more time alone.

The following fall we moved to England, and I escaped the perils of the neighborhood for good. I attended an American school, made new friends, and fell in love with a flirtatious girl from Texas with a lovely southern drawl. After school I would roam the streets of London alone, riding double-decker buses, buying bags of hot chestnuts, drifting through department stores, and then, toward dusk, I would sprint along the streets, jumping over curbstones, dodging businessmen, fire hydrants, old men and women until my eyes, straining in the half-light, became so watery I could not see. Flushed and pleasantly tired I would buy another bag of chestnuts and board another bus, climb to the upper level and sit in my usual seat in the back, by the window. And whether it was because the chestnuts I had bought were still warm, or because my parents had decided for the time being to stay together, or because an ocean finally lay between me and the town I had shared with Billy Purse, I do not know, but as I sat there, looking out onto the lights of an unfamiliar city, I was consumed by a slow and overwhelming sense of well-being, a happiness I had not known in years.

Near
the Flatlands

In the room where we slept, the walls were pale yellow and the trim was bare wood. Across from our beds there was an empty fireplace with small white busts on the mantel, of Tchaikovsky and Beethoven, and a ribbon, red-white-and-blue, with a bronze medallion of a man running, which Richard had won in the hundred-yard dash that fall. On his bureau were postcards, letters, a stack of old coins, and taped to the wall above there was an article entitled "The Night I Was James Bond," with a picture of a man in dark glasses leaning against a wall and holding a cigarette. His clothes sat neatly piled on a chair at the foot of his bed, clean and white and folded. Above the door was one of those old-fashioned fire extinguishers, shaped like a skull and filled with a red liquid that was supposed to drip out in case of fire.

"Why do you suppose they're red?" I asked Richard one night as we lay in our narrow beds, staring up through the dim light. He did not answer. "Richard," I whispered. Light from the street filtered through the curtain, and I could see the curve of his back, and the rise and fall of the covers, and hear the steady sigh of his breathing. I closed my eyes and synchronized my breath with his, in the hope that, by osmosis, I, too, would fall asleep.

We were at the age when boys were supposed to stop being scared of the dark. We were also at the age when boys stopped sleeping in the same bed. Why? I did not understand. I rebelled against this. What was different? And what was different in the way his back moved, breathing in the night? Change came, unspoken, with the silent, unsettling sensation of something I did not yet understand, or feel. I was happy with the way things were. One night at a birthday party for a friend, I found myself sitting on the couch with my arm around a girl I had known since first grade. She was, in my fourteen-year-old eyes, lovely, but I clung to her—my face resting on the nape of her neck, listening to her breath, feeling her hair on my cheek, her warmth—out of no sexual desire: I did not want to kiss her. I walked home that night remembering forgotten insignificant moments from my childhood, and the next day played invented games with a long stick and an old plastic ball, dimly convinced that I had lost something I had always had.

Now, in the morning, I woke early in a room filled with a soft gray light. The covers that lay over Richard's back gently rose and fell. We had spent the night in the same room many times, but it was always I who twitched at the first hint of light, woke, and waited in the still vacuum of morning for him. One summer night my brother and I and Richard agreed to wake at dawn and ride our bikes through the empty, dim-lit streets downtown and eat hot doughnuts. In the morning, my brother and I stood under his window for half an hour, throwing pebbles and sticks, but he would not wake up—he had forgotten.

Downstairs, I could hear his mother knocking around in the kitchen and, from a far corner of the house, a distant torrent of scales from his father's violin. I got dressed quietly and walked across the room to the window. Clouds hung in low, gray shapes over the field, and a soft wind blew down across the meadow to the ocean and the beach. Though it was December, the weather had been warm, and the ground was bare and soft and several trees had budded prematurely. The branches were bare, and swayed gently in the wind. What did they look like with leaves on them? I could not imagine.

In time, Richard woke, we ate, and then stood in the field near his house, watching a small balsa-wood plane he had got for Christmas rise in the wind above the barn, curve, pause, tip its wings, and swoop down again toward the roof, rising in a sudden gust before catching its wings on a branch and falling harmlessly to earth. Though we had not noticed, Richard's father stood on the lawn near the garden, and laughed now, a gentle, rolling laugh, rising in him and making us laugh with him, and then him with us, his laughter fading slowly on his face to a smile. "That was wonderful," he said, his face flushed with cold and his own amusement. His hands were deep in his pockets, and as he stood he seemed, suddenly, like part of the landscape—a tree, the garden—as if he had always been there. "When I was your age, we used to launch planes from up there on the roof," he said, pointing back toward the house, "but they always got caught in that big pine tree and we had to knock them down with sticks. It took forever." He smiled again, and walked slowly back across the lawn toward the house.

That afternoon, Richard and I walk with the plane down across the field toward the beach. A steady breath of wind is coming off the ocean and we have decided to launch the plane from the rocks overlooking the beach. It is low tide, and from the top of the rocks we can see the vast stretch of white sand below, and people walking in the warm winter air. The water is smooth, except for the succession of waves that curl onto the beach, and an occasional ripple spreading itself across the water. The air promises spring. Dogs run in circles, a horse canters in a broken wave, people walk, sounds drift. We stand there briefly, feeling the wind on our faces, wondering which way to launch the plane.

"Fine day for a flight, eh, Watson?" Richard says to me in an affected British accent.

"Quite, Holmes, quite."

"And which way shall we launch her, sire, which way shall we launch her?"

"I think straight, lad, and the wind'll bring her round, down onto the flatlands."

"And how many turns, Watson, how many turns?"

"Oh, I don't know, Holmes. Hundred praps. Praps a hundred and fifty."

"Praps. Hundred and fifty 'tis."

He turns the propeller a hundred and fifty times, and we look out over the beach and at each other.

"Good luck, Watson. Take care."

"And good luck to you, too, Holmes. If anything happens, I'll see you in Singapore on the fifteenth."

"The fifteenth it is, suh. Good luck," Richard says to me, and we shake hands and turn to the sea.

With a practiced hand, he releases the propeller and gives the plane a gentle push toward the ocean. The plane goes straight out from his extended hand, its wings tipping back and forth in the wind, and flies through the air, stringing together a succession of perfect arcs, over the rocks, over the beach, over the breaking waves, straight out to sea. We stand there and stare, until, at last, after what seems a small eternity, the plane arcs toward the water, rises gently in the wind, and settles into the sea.

Richard and I stand there in a brief, dumbstruck silence before turning to each other.

"My God, Holmes," I say. "Congratulations." We shake hands and go scampering down the rocks like two old men who have seen, in the distance, a forgotten love, and remembered.

The Cushion of Time

As a child, I lived with a heightened awareness of my fluctuating moods—the sudden shifts and vacillations of my emotional weather. In third grade, for the first time, I had become aware of myself as a separate, independent being, and was in the habit of observing myself, as if from some high and distant vantage point.

"Am I happy?" I would ask as I walked along through fallen leaves, the warm October sun collapsing onto my back, the weight of my school books tugging on my arm, the mournful cry of a dog's bark rising over the roofs of the small New England town, descending like an answer: "No, no, no!" A poor grade on a math test, a pointless scuffle with one of my siblings, a book report—assigned three weeks before, due the next day, and not yet begun—all gave my world a somber, colorless complexion, and stood between me and what I had imagined as a night spent in front of the television set, falling into a deep and irreverent sleep before being carried up to bed.

But the biggest obstacle to my happiness in those days, was my guitar lesson, a frightening event that took place every Thursday afternoon in a Baptist church in a neighboring town. For a long and painful half hour I would sit in a still and overheated room under the dull, watchful gaze of Mr. DiCarlo, my mentor, whose two hazel eyes swam like fish in the twin aquariums of his round, thick glasses.

"You have not practiced much, have you?" he would ask in his heavy Cuban accent, his impatience measured out by the tapping of his shiny, black shoe.

"Not too much," I offered diplomatically, as a kind of compromise. My palms were beginning to sweat, and I stared sadly down at the music stand where an incomprehensible string of notes danced across the page in a long wavering line, taunting me with their mystery, daring to be played. I could feel the pulse rising in my forehead as I inwardly pleaded for divine intervention—an earthquake, or fire drill, or a sudden death in Mr. DiCarlo's family—anything that might intercede, cause the lesson to end prematurely, and allow me to escape the room. On the floor, his own guitar lay in its plush blue-velvet case, like a beautiful woman in coffin. Now and then, after a particulary feeble attempt of mine, he would pick it up and play—his short, plump fingers rendered suddenly light and nimble—gliding across the frets like a man on ice skates—filling the air, and room, and my guilty soul with beautiful sounds. And not only did his playing pierce me but offered respite from my own gropings. I would have gladly listened for the rest of my lesson had not Mr. DiCarlo then woken from his trance, noticed I was still there and, laying the woman back in her coffin, tapped the music stand with his pen and said, "Again, again!" And I, palms sweating anew, started up on my sad and stumbling journey across the page.

Such were my powers of procrastination in those days that I had risen that morning at 5 a.m. and, for the first time all week, picked up my guitar and tried to practice, and rescue myself from shame. But as I sat in my pajamas in the dead quiet of the house, trying to recover from a truncated dream, the gathered weight of my entire family (four people, two cats, one dog) sleeping was too great for me, made the whole project seem useless, absurd, and I was soon collapsing back into bed, resigned to my fate, relishing the final hour before dawn.

"Practice, practice," Mr. DiCarlo said upon parting, rising from his seat, releasing me for another week. I nodded in sullen agreement and stepped lightly from the room, down the hall to where my father, framed in light, was quietly reading. He smiled when he saw me, rose and, perhaps sensing my sudden lightness and relief, led me out by the hand of forgiveness, tolerance, and drove me home. There I finally did settle in before the glowing television, trying to forget the events of the day, and the lesson to come, from which I seemed protected by a vast cushion of time. But then the next week would arrive after all, and still I had not practiced, and the whole unhappy drama would play itself out again.

Thus, my life traveled its strange, uneven course—a slow and solitary trek across the desert of the school year, punctuated by the weekly terror of my lesson. My parents were of the permissive generation of child-rearing, reluctant both to chastise or to praise, and so I was allowed to continue on my haphazard way unchecked. And although I was generally considered a "happy child," my happiness was transient, volatile, and I was troubled by my inability to become the master of my own moods, harness my happiness, catch it like a wild bird and make it the medium—constant and never ending—in which I lived my life. Instead, I rode a kind of emotional roller coaster marked by sudden shifts of mood and spirit, all brought on by things seemingly beyond my control: a predicted and longed-for snowstorm that had veered from the coast at the last minute and turned to rain; an imperfect haircut which, for an entire week, earned me the derision of my peers; the weekly cycles of procrastination, fear, and moments of fleeting euphoria brought on by my lessons. I came to welcome anything that brought change or novelty to my life, disrupted the texture of my existence, and so I was happy that fall to learn that my grandparents were to come and spend a week with us while my parents were away in the Caribbean.

The week of their arrival it was late fall, or early winter—that precious cusp between Thanksgiving and Christmas when everything in a small New England town seems heightened, suspended in anticipation of the season: the trees are leafless and bare, the sky is a low and glowering gray, the earth in the backyard is hard and unyielding, frozen each night and each day thawed by a tentative, yellow sun. Downtown the Christmas lights are already hung up, suspended between the poles, but even they seem premature, like a celebration before it is entirely justified.

My grandparents arrived at dusk after their eight-hour

drive from Pennsylvania, and we all ran out to the car and ushered them back to the house, like envoys. The following morning we kissed my parents good-bye, and when we returned from school that afternoon they were gone, replaced by older, mysterious presences. From upstairs I could hear a collage of unfamiliar sounds: floorboards creaking, doors closing, water running, the slow, deliberate steps as my grandmother moved around above me. My grandfather was nowhere to be found, and when . asked her where he was she told me, to my surprise, that he had taken it upon himself to attend a parents "open house" at my school—an event my own parents always tried to avoid.

I went across the street to play with a friend, and when I returned my grandfather was sitting at the kitchen table reading the newspaper, wrapping and unwrapping a leash around his broad, speckled hand. He was a tall, well-built man whose pants seemed to hang from somewhere near the center of his body, his belt pulled a notch tighter than his girth, and of our four grandparents he had always been our favorite—not because we didn't love the others, but simply because he was more accessible, and had a way of speaking to children as though we were his superiors, or equals, as if our opinions and views of the world were just as valid as his own. In summer, in his native Pennsylvania, we loved to join him on the long, gentle walks he would take with the dogs, up along the road that ran between the rows of corn and strawberries and potatoes that grew in the rust-red fields. As we walked, pausing now and then as the dog stopped by a bush, or pole, he would carry on a steady conversation with us, his stories punctuated by waves of laughter that seemed to rise over him of their own accord. "God, that was comical," he would say, gazing out across the fields, as if peering into his own past.

Now, as he sat, he was wearing a heavy black coat and one of those innocuous wool hats, pulled tight over his head, that he liked to call "idiot's delight." When we asked him why he said, "Because only an idiot would wear one," which confused us, because it suggested that he thought himself an idiot.

"That's some teacher you've got there," he said when he saw me, looking up. "If I had had a teacher like that I might have really amounted to something. And she had nothing but kind words to say about you—not just your school work, but how well you get along with some of the other students, who aren't, you know, so bright. It's a real credit to your parents, the way they raised you kids. I'm proud as the dickens of all of you—the whole darn family."

When I remarked that he must have also done a great job raising my father, who raised us, he only smiled and said, "No, no. We didn't raise your father. He raised us. He's been an adult from birth. He made us grow up out of shame."

When we visited in summer there was often not enough room in the house, and so my grandfather would volunteer to sleep in the top part of the barn, claiming he was more comfortable among the animals. Once or twice I had slept there with him, in a bed of my own, and as I lay I was impressed by the darkness, the murmur of pigeons in the loft above, the smell of hay, the shuffling and stirring of the horse George in the stable below. Pinholes of light, like constellations of stars, showed through the roof above, and as I lay listening to the deep, steady cadence of my grandfather's breathing, it occurred to me that he was one of the animals after all, only older and wiser than the rest. In the morning, when I woke, the big empty spaces of the barn flooded with a soft, milky light; I looked over for him but he was already gone, stepping out at the first pale hint of day.

My parents were still young and beautiful, and in an odd kind of way they seemed more like my peers to me than my parents. My grandparents were older, clearly of another time and place, and there was something about being with my grandfather that made the world seem safer, more stable, as if in his presence I was protected, shielded from the vicissitudes of life. And in other ways, he had always assumed a more paternal role than my parents: he had written me a letter of praise when he learned I had gotten all A's on my report card; it had been he who, a summer or two before, had bought me my first baseball glove and in our backyard tossed me a softball several times in a soft, underhand arc, until one of his throws missed my glove entirely and collided with my forehead. My grandfather considered it a throwing error, and admonished himself for days.

That night my grandmother cooked dinner for us, the same food we always ate but different in some ineffable way—texture and consistency and the way it looked on the plate—that we did not find entirely appetizing. She had been an only child, had had only one child herself, and so it was perhaps natural that she was less comfortable in her role as surrogate parent than her husband. One night that week I walked into her bedroom when she was only half dressed and upon seeing me she let out a shriek of terror, turned red in the face, and continued to stare at me until I retreated to some safer corner of the house.

And that first weekend I asked her if I could sleep over at a friend's house—Neddy Sherrill's—but she thought I had said "Nettie," a girl's name, became flustered and confused, and told me to ask my grandfather. He straightened out the mystery for me, and drove me over to Neddy's house; on the way home the following day we stopped at the paper store to buy a copy of the evening edition, and when we went in I was surprised to discover that my grandfather knew all the old men there by name.

"Evening gentlemen," he said as we walked in. "I assume you all know my grandson, Pete. Jim's oldest son." And although I knew all these men by face I had never actually heard their names. "Mr. Lena, Mr. Hamill, and . . . er, let's see, Mr. Toomer. Have I got that right? That's one thing you learn as a schoolteacher: names. If you don't, it's bedlam. Bedlam," he repeated solemnly, shaking his head, as if in true recognition of the word. He was a high-school math teacher, and at the end of the year assembly, we were told, he always got the loudest applause.

"Predicting snow, for the end of the week," one of the men said absentmindedly. "Could be a big one."

"Is that right?" said my grandfather. "Well, a little snow never hurt anyone. As long as it's white, it's all the same to me. Well, we'd better get going. His grandmother will be waiting." As we drove home I asked him how he knew all these men.

"Well, I dropped in this morning when I walked the

dog. That's quite a man, Mr. Toomer. His son is the superintendent of schools over in Harrington."

"Hamilton, you mean?"

"That's right, Hamilton. And Mr. Lena was the dogcatcher. Retired. But all of them are real gen-el-men. Real gen-el-men," he said, slowly smiling, revealing his smooth and oddly perfect teeth: in summer, he couldn't eat corn on the cob like the rest of us, but had to saw the kernels off with his knife into a small pile in the middle of his plate. "Teeth wouldn't stand for it," he had explained.

And whether it was the possibility of snow, or the subtle shift of climate my grandparents brought to the house, or the steady stream of praise my grandfather bestowed upon me and my siblings, I do not know, but something that week induced me, for the first time in my musical career, to practice. The song I had been trying to master for weeks had a lovely, melancholy melody which, once it caught hold, would not let go. One day after school I went up to my room, closed the door, and played the same string of notes over and over and over in a sudden desire, or need, to get it right—release the sweetness from the page. When I emerged from my room an hour later, my fingers sore from their exertions, my grandfather was sitting at the kitchen table, reading the paper. He made the room look small.

"That's wonderful," he said when he saw me. "If I had your talent I'd be the happiest man alive. You really make that guitar sing." This, too, came as a surprise, as it was something I had never heard from either my parents or from Mr. DiCarlo. "No, no," he said solemnly. "You've got a real talent for music."

Later that night I watched the news to verify the man's remark, but all the weatherman did was point to a "low pressure system" in the Gulf of Mexico and promised to keep his "eye on it." And I, having a deep distrust in weathermen, knowing they would rather disappoint a few thousand schoolchildren than the few people who didn't like snow—postmen and traveling salemen and old people on crutches—was skeptical, reluctant to believe it until it was almost certain. But once the seed had been planted it would not leave, and as the week slowly passed I became a kind of weatherman myself, studying the sky and clouds and wind, listening to my grandfather's car radio and the murmurings of old men who, it seemed, had nothing better to do than stand around ruminating on the coming storms.

At school that week, my life went on as usual. My teacher, Mrs. Fisher, a young, pretty woman with a head full of blond curls, was as full of praise for my grandfather as he had been of her. That year my childhood ebullience was held in check by my recent discovery of success, and a desire to do well—reap a crop of A's and B's and thereby win the praise and admiration of the world. I had also discovered women, and had become addicted to the little jolt of excitement I would get when the girl in front of me, Debbie Veen, would turn around and ask for a pencil or eraser, or the correct answer to number twelve, and for a moment I could look into her soft, brown eyes, the freckles that laced her cheeks like snow, the precious, wavering line of her pretty pink lips. One day that week she had asked me to meet her behind an old delapidated shed we both passed on the way home from school. Though I didn't understand the request I agreed, and found her there in the shadows, standing near a pile of decaying leaves.

"What?" I said impatiently, annoyed by the mystery of it all. But she answered by wrapping her arms around my head and planting a wet, impulsive kiss somewhere in the vicinity of my mouth. I extracted myself and fled—less in revulsion than out of fear I could not live up to her hopes and expectations. I walked slowly home in a kind of sweet emotional torment, aware that a whole new realm of experience had opened up before me, and was relived to get back to the house, where expectations were clearer.

That afternoon my grandfather and my brother and I took a long walk with the dog, up the hill to Baker's pond on which a smooth skin of ice had formed in the gathering cold. From the frozen mud my brother and I kicked loose sticks and stones and threw them skidding across the ice, or rising—in arcing parabolas above us, drifting downward, landing on the ice with a satisfying thud, and sending an unearthly sound up into the trees, like the cry of a dying whale. The air was still, and the bare black branches of the trees hung motionless against a cold, gray sky. Although my brother and I were natural antagonists, there was something about being with my grandfather that humbled us into not fighting, as if it would make us both unworthy of his praise. Instead, a calm peace had come between us, and we were relieved, for the time being, of the burden of being ourselves.

The dog strained against the leash toward the woods, but my grandfather, adapting the technique he used with his own dog in Pennsylvania, leaned backward and carried on a steady conversation with the dog.

"Easy boy, easy," he said. "I know how you feel—believe me, I do. Sometimes you just have to go, we all do. Easy boy, easy," he repeated and, as if the panting dog somehow understood, the leash went slack between them.

All week long I continued to practice my guitar, and watch the weather reports. And all week long the weathermen continued to give the same uncertain story—hedged predictions and a transparent sense of urgency, all couched in elaborate explanations and atmospheric jargon. By chance the snow was supposed to start on the day of my lesson, setting off in me a web of conflicting emotions: although I was longing for the storm, and for school to be called off, for once I had practiced and was not eager for my lesson to be canceled, as it might somehow diminish my triumph.

The night it was supposed to fall I watched Don Kent—the most trustworthy, I thought, of all the weathermen—as he drew a wonderful puffy bank of clouds with a piece of chalk somewhere off the coast of the Carolinas, and explained how two conflicting fronts—one hot, the other cold—would converge, create atmospheric unrest, and, should all go according to plan, bring us the promised storm. That night I dreamed of snow—dreamed I was kneeling on my bed and looking out the window onto a world of a smooth, impossible whiteness. But when I actually did wake, and knelt on the bed before dawn, I could see in the pale light of the moon that it had not snowed and showed no indication of doing so.

Later, from my usual seat in class, my attention shifted between the shiny brown hair of Debbie Veen and the window: the sky was a dull but hopeful gray; the air cool and still; the ground frozen hard, waiting to be buried. Even my classmates were abuzz with expectation, certain school would be canceled for the following day. But by the afternoon the first flake had still not fallen, and I could picture the cherubic face of Don Kent as he smilingly explained how the storm had veered from the coast at the last minute and, luckily, spared us its wrath. And I did not run home as I usually did on the day of my lesson, but skulked along in a kind of bitter cloud, now and then squinting up through the trees.' On the ride to my lesson my despondency grew, so that even my grandfather couldn't cheer me.

"Why do you suppose it hasn't started yet?" I asked.

"The clouds are slow today. It's a long trip up the coast. Don't worry. It will come. I can feel it in my bones."

And when Mr. DiCarlo's prize pupil—a gangly boy with glasses and long delicate fingers, and the smug, satisfied look of near-genius—emerged from the room, and Mr. DiCarlo waved me inward, thoughts of snow dissipated, replaced by the flow of emotions that usually overcame me in the lightless, dustless room, where every audial imperfection was amplified, reverberating between the walls before finding its way into Mr. DiCarlo's hoary ears. For once the room was not hot, and I was not scared, and my palms did not sweat: instead my fingers were cold, so when I began to play the result was not the little haunting melody with which I had fallen in love, but some imposter, something less certain and sure. But the fact that I had practiced at all was not lost on Mr. DiCarlo. "See what happens when you practice a little," he said. "See? And now that you have learned the notes, maybe we can try for a little music," as if what I had been

playing was something else. He took the beautiful woman
from her coffin and showed me how the melody was supposed to bend and flow and work its way toward a sad
little crescendo at the end—the supreme moment of pathos, or joy. Under his gaze I played it again and again
until, on my final try, I did not pause or stumble: and
perhaps it was my disappointment in the storm, reborn
as beauty, that lent to the music a little spark of life and
made it sound, after all, like music.

"See what happens when you practice?" he repeated
on our way down the hall, his plump hand riding my
back like a small, furry animal. "See?"

My grandfather was not where my father usually was,
and we found him in the office engaged in an animated
discussion with Mrs. Morgan, the director of the music
school—a short, stocky woman with butterfly glasses and
a head of dyed blond curls.

"Well, you've got a great thing going here," he was
telling her. "I've always wanted to play an instrument.
The trombone, or clarinet, or something, but I have ears
of stone. All they can hear is screaming high-school students and falling pennies . . . and, ah, Peter's guitar playing," he added, turning to us.

"How do you do? I'm Pete's grandfather. Pleased to
meet you," He reached out to shake Mr. DiCarlo's hand.
"You've really got that kid playing. You must have a talent for motivation. And that's the hardest thing in the
world, too—getting people to do what's good for them.
I never could, and I've been trying for thirty-five years.
It's a rare gift."

Mr. DiCarlo smiled at the compliment, and it was only
then that I realized the two men—so different in my view

of the world—had something in common after all: false teeth.

"He's quite a man," my grandfather said to me when we were back in the car, pulling out from the parking lot onto the main road. "Mrs. Morgan was telling me something about him. He was a concert musician in Cuba, and when Castro came into power he had to get up and go in a hurry. He's been supporting himself ever since by lessons."

Outside, the last light of day sifted down through the trees, and I looked out through the window across the barren, snowless fields. My grandfather reached down and turned a switch, and with a soft roar the car filled with warm, rushing air. As we swung past the church and the village green the lowering dusk was broken by the Christmas lights of the town—arcs of blue and green and red, and for an instant I caught a sudden, intoxicating whiff of Christmas, and intimations of things to come. We stopped at the paper store and I sat in the car with the engine running and waited for my grandfather, who came out laughing softly at something one of the men had said. When we headed uptown I noticed for the first time that our head-lights weren't on.

"I must be getting senile," he said, and when he turned them on I caught a glimpse of something white—a flash reaching upward, rising and falling in the twin cones of our headlights, forming swirling, serpentine trails in the wake of passing cars. My grandfather eased off the accelerator, and leaned slightly forward in his seat, like the captain of a ship heading into high seas. "I might be an old fool," he said, "but I know snow when I see it, and this is it. It's really going to happen."

I did not know whether the few flakes that were falling signified that the awaited storm had come at last or simply that, on its way out to sea, it was giving us a taste of what might have been, but for once it did not seem to matter. My happiness was intact, complete, and in the course of the week I had learned that the deceits and uncertainties of the world beyond were sometimes less important than what I hoped for and believed.

Summer

───────────

I t was the first week in August, the time when summer
briefly pauses, shifting between its beginning and its
end: the light had not yet begun to change, the leaves
were still full and green on the trees, the nights were still
warm. From the woods and fields came the hiss of crick-
ets; the line of distant mountains was still dulled by the
edge of summer haze, the echo of fireworks was replaced
by the rumble of thunder and the hollow premonition of
school, too far off to imagine though dimly, dully felt.
His senses were consumed by the joy of their own fulfillment: the satisfying swat of a tennis ball, the dappled
damp and light of the dirt road after rain, the alternating
sensations of sand, mossy stone, and pine needles under
bare feet. His days were spent in the adolescent pursuit
of childhood pleasures: tennis, a haphazard round of golf,
a variant of baseball adapted to the local geography: two

pine trees as foul poles, a broomstick as the bat, the apex
of the small, secluded house the dividing line between
home runs and outs. On rainy days they swatted bottle
tops across the living room floor, and at night vented
budding cerebral energy with games of chess thoughtfully
played over glasses of iced tea. After dinner they would
paddle the canoe to the middle of the lake and drift beneath the vast, blue-black dome above them, looking at
the stars and speaking softly in tones which, with the
waning summer, became increasingly philosophical: the
sky's blue vastness, the distance and magnitude of stars,
an endless succession of numbers, gave way to a rising
sensation of infinity, eternity, an imagined universe with
no bounds. But the sound of the paddle hitting against
the side of the canoe, the faint shadow of surrounding
mountains, the cry of a nocturnal bird brought them back
to the happy, cloistered finity of their world, and they
paddled slowly home and went to bed.

Homer woke to the slant and shadow of a summer
morning, dressed in their shared cabin, and went into
the house where Mrs. Thyme sat alone, looking out
across the flat, blue stillness of the lake. She poured him
a cup of coffee and they quietly talked, and it was then
that his happiness seemed most tangible. In this summer
month with the Thymes, freed from the complications
of his own family, he had released himself to them and,
as interim member—friend, brother, surrogate son—he
lived in a blessed realm between two worlds.

From the cool darkness of the porch, smelling faintly of
moldy books and kerosene and the tobacco of burning
pipes, he sat looking through the screen to the lake, shim-

mering beneath the heat of a summer afternoon: a dog lay sleeping in the sun, a bird hopped along a swaying branch, sunlight came in through the trees and collapsed on the sandy soil beside a patch of moss, or mimicked the shade and cadence of stones as they stepped to the edge of a lake where small waves lapped a damp rock and washed onto a sandy shore. An inverted boat lay decaying under a tree, a drooping American flag hung from its gnarled pole, a haphazard dock started out across the cove toward distant islands through which the white triangle of a sail silently moved.

The yellowed pages of the book from which he occasionally read swam before him: ". . . Holmes clapped the hat upon his head. It came right over the forehead and settled on the bridge of his nose. 'It is a question of cubic capacity' said he . . ." Homer looked up. The texture of the smooth, unbroken air was cleanly divided by the sound of a slamming door, echoing up into the woods around him. Through the screen he watched Fred's sister Sandra as she came ambling down the path, stepping lightly between the stones in her bare feet. She held a towel in one hand, a book in the other, and wore a pair of pale blue shorts—faded relics of another era. At the end of the dock she stopped, raised her hands above her head, stretching, and then sat down. She rolled over onto her stomach and, using the book as a pillow, fell asleep.

Homer was amused by the fact that although she did this every day, she didn't get any tanner. When she first came in her face was faintly flushed, and there was a pinkish line around the snowy band where her bathing suit strap had been, but the back of her legs remained an endearing, pale white, the color of eggshells, and her back acquired only the softest, brownish blur. Sometimes she kept her shoes on, other times a shirt, or sweater, or just collapsed onto the seat of the boat, her pale eyelids turned upward toward the pale sun; and then, as silently as she arrived, she would leave, walking back through the stones with the same, casual sway of indifference. He would watch her, hear the distant door slam, the shower running in the far corner of the house; other times he would just look up and she would be gone.

On the tennis court she was strangely indifferent to his heroics. When the crucial moment arrived—Homer serving in the final game of the final set—the match would pause while she left, walking across the court, stopping to call the dog, swaying out through the gate. Homer watched her as she went down the path—her pale legs in the mottled light—and, impetus suddenly lost, he double faulted, stroked a routine backhand over the back fence, and the match was over.

When he arrived back at the house she asked him who won, but didn't seem to hear his answer. "I wish I could go sailing," she said, looking distractedly out over the lake.

At night, when he went out to the cottage where he and Fred slept, he could see her through the window as she lay on her bed, reading, her arm folded beneath her head like a leaf. Her nightgown, pulled and buttoned to her chin, pierced him with a regret that had no source or resolution, and its imagined texture floated in the air above him as he lay in bed at night, suspended in the surrounding darkness, the scent of pine, the hypnotic cadence of his best friend's breathing.

Was it that he had known her all his life, and as such

had grown up in the shadow of her subtle beauty? Was it the condensed world of the lake, the silent reverence of surrounding woods, mountains, which heightened his sense of her and brought the warm glow of her presence into soft, amorous focus? She had the hair of a baby, the freckles of a child, and the sway of motherhood. Like his love, her beauty rose up in the world that spawned and nurtured it, and found in the family the medium in which it thrived, and in Homer distilled to a pure distant longing for something he had never had.

One day they climbed a mountain, and as the components of family and friends strung out along the path on their laborious upward hike, he found himself tromping along through the woods with her with nobody else in sight. Now and then they would stop by a stream, or sit on a stump, or stone, and he would speak to her, and then they would set off again, he following her. But in the end this day exhausted him, following her pale legs and tripping sneakers over the ruts and stones and a thousand roots, all the while trying to suppress a wordless, inarticulate passion, and the last mile or so he left her, sprinting down the path in a reckless, solitary release, howling into the woods around him. He was lying on the grass, staring up into the patterns of drifting clouds when she came ambling down. "Wher'd you go? I thought I'd lost you," she said, and sat heavily down in the seat of the car. On the ride home, his elbow hopelessly held in the warm crook of her arm, he resolved to release his love, give it up, on the grounds that it was too disruptive to his otherwise placid life. But in the days to follow he discovered that his resolution had done little to change her, and her life went on its oblivious, happy course without him.

His friendship with Fred, meanwhile, continued on its course of athletic and boyhood fulfillment. Alcohol seeped into their diet, and an occasional cigarette, and at night they would drive into town, buy two enormous cans of Australian beer and sit at a small cove by the lake, talking. One night on the ride home Fred accelerated over a small bridge, and as the family station wagon left the ground their heads floated up to the ceiling, touched, and then came crashing down as they landed, and Fred wrestled the car back onto course. Other times they would take the motorboat out onto the lake and make sudden racing turns around buoys, sending a plume of water into the air and everything in the boat, including them, crashing to one side. But always with these adventures Homer felt a pang of absence, and was always relived when they headed back toward the familiar cove, and home.

As August ran its merciless succession of beautiful days, Sandra drifted in and out of his presence in rising oscillations of sorrow and desire. She worked at a bowling alley on the other side of the lake, and in the evening Homer and Fred would drive the boat over, bowl a couple of strings, and wait for her to get off work. Homer sat at the counter and watched her serve up sloshing cups of coffee, secretly loathing the leering gazes of whiskered truck drivers, and loving her oblivious, vacant stare in answer, hip cocked, hand on counter, gazing up into the neon air above their heads. When she was finished, they would pile into the boat and skim through darkness the four or five miles home, and it was then, bundled beneath

sweaters and blankets, the white hem of her waitressing
dress showing through the darkness, their hair swept in
the wind and their voices swallowed by the engine's slow,
steady growl, that he felt most powerless to her attraction.
As the boat rounded corners he would close his eyes and
release himself to gravity, his body's warmth swaying into
hers, guising his attraction in the thin veil of centrifugal
force. Now and then he would lean into the floating
strands of her hair and speak into her fragrance, watching
her smile swell in the pale half-light of the moon, the
amber glow of the boat's rear light, her laughter spilling
backward over the swirling "V" of wake.

Into the humid days of August a sudden rain fell, leaving
the sky a hard, unbroken blue and the nights clear and
cool. In the morning when he woke, leaving Fred a heap
of sighing covers in his bed, he stepped out into the first
rays of sunlight that came through the branches of the
trees and sensed, in the cool vapor that rose from damp
pine needles, the piercing cry of a blue jay, that something had changed. That night as they ate dinner—ham-
burgers and squash and corn on the cob—everyone wore
sweaters, and as the sun set behind the undulating line
of distant mountains—burnt, like a filament of summer
into his blinking eyes—it was with an autumnal tint, a
reddish glow. Several days later the tree at the end of the
point bloomed with a sprig of russet leaves, one or two
of which occasionally fell, and their lives became filled
with an unspoken urgency. Life of summer went on in
the silent knowledge that, with the slow, inexorable see-
page of an hourglass, it was turning into fall. Another
mountain was climbed, annual tennis matches were ar-

ranged and played. Homer and Fred became unofficial champions of the lake by trouncing the elder Dewitt boys, unbeaten in several years. "Youth, youth," glum Billy Dewitt kept saying over iced tea afterward, in jest, though Homer could tell he was hiding some greater sense of loss.

And the moment, the conjunction of circumstance that, through the steady exertion of will, minor adjustments of time and place, he had often tried to induce, never happened. She received his veiled attentions with a kind of amused curiosity, as if smiling back on innocence. One night they had been the last ones up, and there was a fleeting, shimmering moment before he stepped through the woods to his cabin and she went to her bed that he recognized, in a distant sort of way, as the moment of truth. But to touch her, or kiss her, seemed suddenly incongruous, absurd, contrary to something he could not put his finger on. He looked down at the floor and softly said good night. The screen door shut quietly behind him and he went out into the darkness and made his way through the unseen sticks and stones, and it was only then, tripping drunkenly on a fallen branch, that he realized he had never been able to imagine the moment he distantly longed for.

The Preacher gave a familiar sermon about another summer having run its course, the harvest of friendship reaped, and a concluding prayer that, "God willing, we will all meet again in June." That afternoon Homer and Fred went sailing, and as they swept past a neighboring cove Homer saw in its sullen shadows a girl sitting alone in a canoe, and in an eternal, melancholy signal of parting, she waved to them as they passed. And there was something in the way that she raised her arm which, when added to the distant impression of her fullness, beauty, youth, filled him with desire but their boat moved inexorably past anyway, slapping the waves, and she disappeared behind a crop of trees.

The night before they were to leave they were all sitting in the living room after dinner—Mrs. Thyme sewing, Fred folded up with the morning paper, Homer reading on the other end of the couch where Sandra was lying—when the dog leapt up and things shifted in such a way that Sandra's bare foot was lightly touching Homer's back. Mrs. Thyme came over with a roll of newspaper, hit the dog on the head and he leapt off. But to Homer's surprise Sandra's foot remained, and he felt, in the faint sensation of exerted pressure, the passive emanation of its warmth, a distant signal of acquiescence. And as the family scene continued as before it was with the accompanying drama of Homer's hand, shielded from the family by a haphazard wall of pillows, migrating over the couch to where, in a moment of breathless abandon, settled softly on the cool hollow of her arch. She laughed at something her mother had said, her toe twitched, but her foot remained. It was only then, in the presence of the entire family, that he realized she was his accomplice, and that, though this was as far as it would ever go, his love had been returned.

Out on the Marsh

I turned twenty-one a month or two ago, and I have been rather surprised lately to find myself suddenly conscious of my age. Twenty-one: that sounds very different from twenty right now, though I don't think I would have thought so a year ago. Against my better judgment, I now think of myself as standing at the edge of what presents itself as "the rest of my life," the previous twenty years being some sort of vague and distant warm-up. I am suddenly aware, I suppose, that my present actions are an indicator, a preview, of what's to come. I feel old.

At night, sitting under the dim yellow light of my desk lamp, I take from my wallet two photographs, from expired driver's licenses, of me at sixteen and at twenty. My hair has grown, my cheeks have broadened. Do I look older? Have I lost the question in my eye? I am handsome,

I am told; I smile and look away. This picture of me at sixteen was on my first license, and I have always liked it. At the registry of motor vehicles, when it came time to turn my license in for a new one, I told the woman at the desk that I wanted to keep the picture, and she took a pair of large scissors, snipped it brusquely from the rest, and tossed it onto her desk with a flip of her chubby wrist. I have kept it with me since.

Have I become more sedate lately? I am home from college for spring vacation and spend my days puttering around the house and taking long solitary walks on the marsh with Mtoti, my dog. He has recently become my best friend, and I must admit I find his company entirely sufficient. A large red-haired golden retriever, he walks with a sway that suggests he should not eat so much. The other day we found a deer carcass, completely decomposed except for the fur and a foot, which he tried to sneak away from me to eat in the woods. I went after him and got the foot and threw it into the creek, only to have him grunt and grovel and wheeze in a vain and pathetic search through the mud. He walked right over it twice, but could not see or smell it through the water, so I pointed it out to him with a long stick, and he stole away with it back to the house and finished it under a tree on the lawn.

It is on these recent wanderings that I have become acquainted with Mr. Birch, not so much in conversation as by seeing him, a familiar, waving figure on the marsh—a mobile landmark—at all hours of the day, collecting old scraps of wood, gazing toward the horizon. He lives here on the marsh with his wife, along the road that runs from town to the ocean, in a small white house on a knoll hidden in the trees. They are both in their eighties, and in the winter, when the tide is high and the wind blows from the northeast, the neighbors worry for them, knowing that the road to their house is covered with water and the knoll the house sits on has become an island. But when the tide subsides, and we hurry over to see if everything is all right, we find them, invariably, fine, surprised and amazed by our concern.

Now and then the paths of our wanderings intersect, and Mr. Birch and I stand together briefly, looking out over the marsh, trying to think of things to say. I ask him questions mostly, about the weather or the birds, and he returns short, soft-spoken answers, and we set off on our different ways, glad to have had someone to talk to, relieved to be again alone. It is his distant presence I cherish most—the sight of his ancient and erect form gliding across the marsh in his aluminum motorboat, his arm raised in a wave, his collar flapping in the wind—and the sense that all I see and hear and love here is shared.

Mr. Birch spends much of his time working in the small yard next to his house. The other day, after watching him and Mrs. Birch climb into their tired green Rambler and drive over the bridge toward town, I walked up to the house and stood in the yard. I was struck there by the wonderful haphazard order of the objects he has collected and saved and arranged in a randomness I knew not to be random—a disorder I thought to be the highest form of order, a personal one, which only Mr. Birch understands. A buoy hangs by a rope from a lilac bush. The wheelbarrow is concealed, covered by a heavy piece of gray canvas, faded by the sun. Stumps double as stools, clothespins cling like birds to the line, a mattress dries in the sun. The grass is full but matted, padded by his step, and a beaten path bends through a gap in the bushes, marking his daily route between the house and the yard, between the yard and the marsh. I wonder if it has ever occurred to him that he alone has made this track—years of work, three decades of soft steps. Or at his age do you take these things for granted?

I met him recently on the road in front of his house and he pointed out two pine trees, forty feet high, that he and his wife planted from pots when they first moved here. We stood there marveling at their height, and I— and Mr. Birch, too, perhaps, as he leaned over to pet the dog —thought of what these trees implied about his age. It was a beautiful spring day, with a high, cool wind blowing through the tops of the trees. We said good-bye and I walked slowly over the bridge back toward my house. I had been out on the marsh for several hours that day, and Mtoti was tired and followed a few feet behind me. I turned to him and ran backwards, urging him on, clapping my hands, calling his name, and he worked himself into a run. On the lawn we stopped, and I bent down to hug him. In the afternoon light, I could see that the gray flecks of his muzzle had gone to white, and I realized that he had drifted into old age without my having noticed. I have thought of him all these years as my peer, but it is only now, in the blue light of spring, that I realize he has grown old without me.

Apples

My mother is alone in the kitchen. Everyone else has eaten and the table is scattered with sections of the Sunday paper and half-finished cups of coffee. She is standing at the sink washing dishes and turns to me when I enter. In the soft morning light, I think she is beautiful. She cooks an egg for me and heats the coffee. I thank her as she pours two cups and sits down. She lights a cigarette, holding it high in the air with a cocked wrist; I watch the ribbon of blue smoke drift through a dense slant of light that falls in through the window.

I eat my egg and we talk. How is school? What did you do last night? Have you talked to your father recently? My brother has called from his college in Minnesota. He sounds depressed, she says, and has taken up parachuting. We laugh. He has a new girlfriend—someone from Maryland who is in a motorcycle gang—and she might

come home with him for Christmas. I wonder aloud if
he is flunking out, but my mother doesn't think so. And
. . . she talked to Ann, my older sister, and she is fine,
and is coming over for dinner with her husband, Bill. My
sister Katharine has gone to the store; Peter, her boyfriend, is coming out on the one-o'clock train; Dad is
coming over to help put away the tennis court and is
going to stay for dinner. And . . . I guess that is all the
news, she says. Huh? When is Dad coming? Well, he said
around noon, so any second now. She clears the table
of the cups of tepid coffee, puts on her coat, and steps
out the door. She sticks her head back through—"I'll be
out raking leaves if you want me." She smiles. "O.K.," I
answer. "Have fun."

I never know quite what to do with myself on these
Sundays when I come home from college. I usually bring
a friend, but no one could come this time. The book I
am supposed to read is too long and boring and I am not
far enough behind in my work to start doing it on
Sundays.

I put on a jacket and walk out into the cool fall air. It
is my favorite kind of day, cloudy and gray with no chance
of rain or sun. The air is perfectly still and seems to am-
plify every sound. My mother is standing in the middle
of the yard raking leaves. She bends slightly forward from
the waist, making, somehow, her methodical chore look
graceful. I call the dogs, cut through the bushes that
stand between the house and the road, and walk to the
bridge. It is a small road, a dead end, and I wonder if any
cars have been down it this morning. The dogs bound
along the vast stretch of marsh and I stoop to fill my hands
and pockets with the apples that lie by the side of the

road. They are small apples, green, and not good for eating but hard and good for throwing.

The wooden planks of the bridge are wet from dew, and I can see that no cars have been down this morning, after all. I wipe off the top rail and lean out over the water. The tide has turned and flows under the bridge with a soft, insistent gurgle. I toss an apple into the smooth, slow-moving funnel of water upstream and watch its casual drift back toward the bridge. When it is almost under my feet it quickly picks up speed and is lost from sight. I dash to the other rail in time to see it appear, bobbing along in the swift current toward the ocean.

On the far shore, the boat my father bought us several summers ago sits high in the water like a duck. From my pocket I take an apple and, stepping backward, throw it as hard as I can toward the boat. Not hard enough, though, and the apple ends with a splash in the water. Another apple—another throw. Too short this time, a *thwop* in the muddy bank. After several more attempts I launch a perfect arc, a bull's-eye, sending the hollow echo of apple on wood reeling across the soft green marsh. I kick the remaining apples into the water, call the dogs, and walk back to the house.

My yard is shaped like an almond, or a tear. At one end, the trunks of two pear trees have been converted into a soccer goal; from the crossbar—a long pipe painstakingly chosen and extracted from the great collection of wood and metal in the barn—hangs a fishing net I took to be discarded and removed from the refuse of some fishing boats one summer. The net is woven with a rope to the bar, nailed to the tree on both sides, and held to the ground with two-by-fours, making it, as it were, ball tight. When I was in high school, I spent part of every day here, banging balls past a hapless, imaginary goaltender, but now on weekends I try to get my sister to take his place. She is not here now, and the ball floats unimpeded into the net. Henry, my brother, used to play, but in general found me too competitive and preferred long solitary walks on the marsh with a big stick, finding horseshoe crabs and smashing bottles. Whenever a friend came over and we played, I ran the entire time in a desperate attempt to stave off my partner's inevitable, dreaded boredom, which would put a sure stop to the game.

I am standing at the edge of the yard, on the driveway, next to the giant elm with the basketball hoop, the soccer ball at my feet, when I hear the distant rumble of a car. A minute later my father's red Maverick appears from around the corner and glides onto the driveway with the sound of a breaking wave. He takes his hands off the steering wheel, waves to me like a madman with both, and comes to a stop in front of the elm. As he is getting out of the car I send the soccer ball into the air with a flip of my foot and we watch it rise high above the basket, pause at the top of its flight, then drop clean through without a sound. My father is frozen like a statue halfway out the car. He smiles at me and comes back to life. "Amazing," he says, closing the door with a bang. "Just amazing." "I was *trying* to do that, you know," I say, fearing he will think otherwise. "I can't believe it," he says, though I know by the tone of his voice he does.

This is not the first time my father and I have seen a minor miracle. There was a time at dinner when everyone else was struggling with the beef and burnt Yorkshire pudding and my father looked up in time to see me flip a pea into the top of a milk bottle with my knife. My mother and brother and sisters did not understand our glee when we showed them the pea sitting in a puddle of milk at the bottom of the bottle, and went back to their food puzzled and annoyed. But it didn't matter: we knew what had happened.

And it was just last summer that my father whacked a 4-wood into the heart of a lone apple tree in the middle of the fourth fairway at Cape Ann. The Puerto Rican man we had invited to join us on the first hole couldn't believe it when I climbed the tree in search and found nothing but a hole deeper than my arm was long. We shook the tree and paced around for half an hour, but were left only with the conclusion that the ball had gone straight down the hole on a beeline. My father dropped another ball and sliced it into the woods, but it didn't matter. We strode down the fairway with a strange and certain fullness, knowing secretly what the other knew, so nothing need be said.

My father and I have always had a silent rapport, a sympathy with each other that, since he left the house, has come strongly into my memory. I remember driving with him every Tuesday when he would pick me up from school early and take me to my guitar lesson—a frightening event that took place in a dusty Unitarian church several towns away. There we would sit, side by side, moving through winter's early darkness in the heat of the old blue Fairlane. I remember asking him about Hitler and Arnold Palmer and hearing in his reply such a weight, such a casual weight, that I would sink deeper into my seat, wishing secretly that we had farther to go.

He is in the kitchen now, with my mother, drinking coffee and arguing. Their pained voices follow me down the hall and into the study. I slam the door and put on a record. I take a photo album off the shelf and sit down, blocking out the last trace of their words with my thumbs in my ears.

Although it has only been two and a half years, I cannot remember what it was like when my father lived with us. He has assumed a passivity since then, relinquishing his right to give suggestions or advice to his children. When he comes to see us every Sunday he acts like a slightly nervous guest wondering if he is in the right hotel. He walks around the house, out into the yard, fixes a chair with my sister, argues with my mother, carves the chicken, and leaves, stepping meekly out the back door after supper. He always leaves suddenly, catching us with a bite of dessert left on our plates or a swig of coffee in our mouths, and my mother asking, invariably, why so soon. I sympathize with him, though, and would like to reassure him, knowing somehow that his sudden departure is not out of any eagerness to return to his apartment in the city but out of the pain it causes him to stay.

In the photo album I find my mother, twenty years younger, wearing red lipstick and a black beret. She is standing in front of our old house holding the hand of Katharine, age two. It is springtime, and an orange blur, a crocus, is sprouting up from the lifeless dirt behind her. She is smiling. My grandparents' house in Pennsylvania: on the porch a cat stoops, drinking milk next to the lime-stone shadow of the trellis where grapes grow; my grandparents are sitting on the park bench they bought to grow old on under the walnut tree. Me, age five, walking down a long, dusty road in the Caribbean with blue shorts and a broad brown back. My mother, poised between two trees—a statue, overlooking a blue-green sea. Forgotten cars: a blue Falcon and a gray Corvair.

All taken with a Brownie Hawkeye, my mother reminds me as she walks into the room.

"Oh, are you through fighting?" I ask.

"What?" she says incredulously. "We have to talk, don't we?"

"Sure, but if you're going to fight you don't have to subject the whole house to it."

"Oh, piffle," she says, walking out of the room with a sway that suggests I should grow up.

The record is over and I walk into the kitchen—empty; then the TV room. Nothing is on but old movies and bowling. I put on my jacket and walk out the screen door into the yard. I look for the soccer ball, find it in the bushes, and kick it casually into the empty net. It has grown slightly colder, and the sky looks more like snow than like rain. I button the top of my jacket, walk to the goal, and roll the ball out of the net. I hear the screen door clack shut and see my father walk stiffly across the driveway.

His light-blue sweater is worn thin at the elbows and reaches only halfway down his back, hanging there like a limp flag. His hair has become more gray than black since I last saw him, or maybe it is just the light. He smiles. "I couldn't stand the thought of you out here alone," he says, stepping into the worn patch in front of the goal. As if in reply, I knock the ball into a long arc across the yard and into his hands. He rolls it back to me.

"What do you want for Christmas?" he asks, though it is more than a month away.

"I don't care—nothing."

He accepts this as a reasonable answer and we play—I darting about in the waning light, sending shot after shot in toward the two pear trees, and he stiffly erect on the patch of packed earth, stretching for the ball, his knuckles cracking, the knees of his pants caked with dirt. As we play on, the difference in our years dissolves with the simplicity of our opposite, mutually dependent duties, and we become, briefly, peers.

Inexplicably, I remember something my father has told me, something that his father told him, the only advice, his father said, worth giving: always butter your toast toward the edges, because enough always gets in the middle, and whatever happens to you, it will be a new experience. I repeat this to my father. He looks toward the sky and laughs, and as he does so, my shot sails through his thoughts into the upper corner, nicking the side of the tree.

Spring

Shaun woke to the twitter of birds, the sound of footsteps on the rug nearby, the vague impression of light behind his closed, half-sleeping eyes. He opened them to the pale light of morning, a blur of green, the dappled patterns of sun and shade that fell through the trees and landed on the dusty glass of the window. His knees were sore from the rough carpet on which he'd slept, his neck ached, and he could feel the cold trying to work its way under the blanket to his pale skin. He was suspended in the pleasant void between sleeping and waking when he experienced the peculiar sensation of falling snow—something touching the nape of his neck, a shadow skimming across the plush blue of carpet, a blur of white seen in the corner of his eye. He looked up, and there saw the smiling face of she who, looking down on him from the balcony above, was releasing a stream of petals, like a blessing, from her outstretched hand.

"Good morning," she said and smiled, and then was gone.

"Good morning," Shaun answered, suddenly aware of a small, logistical problem: he lay naked under the blanket, his clothes lay in a heap across the floor, she, whom he hardly knew, was on the half floor above him, overlooking the room. His problem was solved a moment later when, using the trick he had learned from his sisters, he draped himself in his blanket, crossed the room, and pulled on his pants beneath it. He put on his shirt, socks, shoes, then walked up the half-flight of stairs to where she was sitting.

"Did you sleep well?" she asked now, as Shaun sat down beside her.

"Yes, thank you." Her voice had a lilting quality, as if the words were being sung, not spoken—an observation verified a moment later by another: when she walked, he noticed, gliding through a beam of sunlight, or skimming across the carpet, she held her arms slightly behind her, and slightly bent, like a bird preparing for flight. She offered him a cup of tea, and after breakfast he gave her a ride into town. She was wearing black Chinese shoes and an unusual squarish hat with floral motives and lots of tiny mirrors sewn into the cloth. Her cheeks were flushed a rosy shade of pink, and when he pulled up in front of the college he felt a strange paternal impulse to kiss her good-bye. He didn't, and she stepped quickly out and walked away. He wasn't even sure of her name: Laura, Laurel, Lauren—he couldn't remember.

That afternoon he was hired by an affable man with a

pony tail as a grounds keeper at the tennis club, and a week later he found a place to live not far away, a room in the house of a friend of a friend.

"That's great," she said when he next saw her, "We should go have a drink to celebrate."

They walked up the street to a small, oriental bar and, before he had had a chance to consider it she had ordered a "Scorpion Bowl," a potent concoction of uncertain ingredients served in a large white bowl with two straws and several floating nasturtiums.

A candle was placed on the table between them, and as the contents of the bowl slowly descended it glowed in increasingly romantic tones. By the time they left, he was drunk. Outside, the air was cooler, the sky blacker, the stars more numerous than he remembered. Now and then a bush in bloom, or a flowering tree, moved toward them in the darkness, and as they paused to inhale its fragrance Shaun had the distinct impression that they were walking onto the set of a play.

"You can sleep in my room, if you want," Laura said when they were inside. She loaned him a pair of pajamas and they lay side by side, reading.

He kissed her lightly on the lips and then fell asleep, her pale, tepid hand folded into his.

His work began at the astounding hour of seven, requiring him to leave her apartment by six, and often, as if in apology for keeping him up late the night before, Laura would get up too, sit with him as he drank a cup of tea and ate a piece of toast, and then kiss him goodbye. Shaun mounted his bike and sped off through the translucent spring air, his wheels humming as they swept faster and faster over the dappled cement, his passing announced by the rising clamor of birds.

When he arrived home in the evenings, he would find little notes written on slips of colored paper, left under a flower pot, or in the crook of two branches, or beside some blooming crocuses, held in place by a shiny black stone. Now and then they contained tangible information, but mostly they were just the scattered lines of childlike poems: "Roses are red, violets are blue, A little red hen is thinking of you." After he washed, changed, and tried to make himself feel as though he really lived there, he would drift down the street, turn in the alley to the backyard and slip in through the sliding glass doors.

At work, carrying heavy bags of clay or punching ventilation holes into the grass courts, pushing an absurdly heavy roller or painting a fence, he would contemplate this love affair in which, through no conscious effort of his own, he suddenly found himself involved. If nothing else, it was unexpected: he had recently disentangled himself from a relationship that had consumed him to the point of exhaustion, and had formed the unhappy focus of all of his thoughts and dreams for an entire year. And when that relationship had finally ended, leaving him a tattered wreck in its wake, he had impulsively left school, drifted around Europe for a month, and then returned; he had imagined a spring devoted to impulse and promiscuity—but through it all had somehow become involved with Laura who, questions of love aside, was eager to go forward, to release herself to whatever hope or promise their sudden union held.

One night at a bar he tried to explain his doubts, his uncertainties, but then forgot what he was saying, or why he was saying it. Once started, though, it was too late to stop, and Laura turned impetuous, angry, sharp. Her ears burned in receipt of Shaun's stumbling message, her hand went limp in his and withdrew.

"I just had a girlfriend," he tried to explain. "And when I met you, I was just planning to be alone for a while."

"So why don't you? Why do you spend so much time with me, if you want to be alone? What am I supposed to do? Hang out until you recover?"

The questions were all good ones, and Shaun had no answers. Her face grew red and hot; her warmth cooled; her supple body turned angular, hard. The aspect of her character revealed through their sudden travails endeared her to him further.

"I still want to be with you, I just . . ."

"Want to keep your distance?"

"No."

"It doesn't work that way, I'm telling you. I've tried it." She leaned toward him across the table, in a gesture of consolation, as if it were *she* who would be leaving him.

These vague discussions interwove themselves into the texture of their previous happiness. He tried to forget ever having raised the subject, but once the seed had been planted it would not go away, and instead grew like a weed between two stones.

One night they went out for coffee, but what he had imagined as reconciliation turned sour when, on the way home, she told him she couldn't see him anymore.

"You should be by yourself for a while, until you figure it out. But I can't help you." It was dark, and they stopped by a streetlight on the corner where she was to turn down to her house and he was to continue, alone, on to his.

He held her lightly by the arms and tried to pull her to
him, but she stood perfectly still, offered no help, and
he let go.

"We're not going to see each other?" he asked,
incredulous.

"Nope." She was not looking at him but past him, her
heel impatiently tapping the pavement. He was amazed
by this, her stoic resistance, and amazed even more
when, a moment later, she turned and walked away. She
was wearing a shiny blue satin jacket, with the single word
"Korea" sewn into the cloth, and it was this single word
that pierced him, glowing dully back at him through the
darkness.

"Laura!" he called weakly after her, but she turned the
corner and was gone.

As he walked home he half expected her to appear on
the street before him, but she didn't—the only sign of
life was a black cat tiptoeing furtively over the curb, leaping up onto a white picket fence and disappearing into
the weeds. He sat out on the front steps of his house,
waiting for the phone to ring, but it didn't ring then, nor
did it ring in the days to follow.

At work his body performed its mundane duties while
his mind raced through the events of their now dissolved
relationship. Like a man chasing a check in a whirlwind
he pursued bits and pieces of information which, once
gathered, he hoped would explain what had happened:
"I cannot be with her because I am not ready; I am not
ready because I am still recovering from another relationship; perhaps in the future . . ." And here the fragile
house of cards—a construct of imperfect logic—was

swept away by a sudden gust of wind, and disappeared on the pale, greenish grass before him.

A truck filled with heavy bags of clay arrived and he spent a couple of days unloading them, spreading the clay with rakes, rolling it flat and smooth. The heavy work was welcome, penance to his confusion, but when it was over, and he trudged tiredly toward the subway, thoughts of her returned. Strange sentences, fragments of sentences, formed in his mouth and were spoken to no one, surprising even their author: "I'm sorry . . ." he heard himself saying as his token fell through the subway slot, and he pushed on through. When he arrived home he would survey the melancholy landscape around his front door for something she might have left, a note of reconciliation or regret, but there was none. The list of reasons why he no longer saw her evolved into an amorphous, unhappy mass, and as he sat at his desk one night, he finally realized she wasn't going to call, and so wrote down a few lines on the back of an envelope: "Dear Laura, I wonder how you spend your nights and days. I will slip this under your door on my way to work. I miss you, would like to visit you soon. . . . Love, S."

The next morning he left it under her door, and then sped quickly off through the still, dawning streets, faster and faster over the cool cement, jumping over curbs, snapping fallen sticks, swerving to avoid cars and school-children and dogs.

At work he was unusually active, starting and starring in a tennis ball war, hoisting several bags of clay at once, but by the end of the day, as he walked toward the subway, he was spent, exhausted. He picked up his bike where he had left it chained to a thin maple, and glided slowly home under a canopy of trees, through neighborhoods filled with children playing games between the passing cars. As he passed one group a tennis ball ricocheted off a car, hopped once, and leapt up before him. Shaun instinctively swung his foot, connected, and to his amusement and the children's shrieks, the ball flew on a lovely parabola up through the branches of the trees and disappeared over a fence.

As he approached his house he slowed and contemplated the possible responses to his note: no answer at all; a short, stern message asking him to leave her alone; any kind of note, short, long, or middling, which by any means allowed him to resume whatever it was they shared—love, lust, confusion—it didn't matter which. These words fell away, like absurd mathematical equations, groping after something pure, intangible, whole. He was prepared for any answer, or none. When he arrived he quickly dismounted, leapt up the front steps, down again, and surveyed the shrubbery, loose stones, drain pipe, for any signs of a response. He pawed through the bushes, lifted a flower pot, then kicked it. He checked the gutter, lifted a brick, clumped up the stairs, looked behind the door, and then went in, collapsing in a despondent heap on his bed.

He could hear his own heart beating and, from across the hall, the collage of sounds that signaled the waking of his roommate, a pale nocturnal creature who worked in an all night parking garage: the rasp of the alarm, a creaking bed, footsteps, running water, gargle, the rasp of an electric razor, more footsteps, and then a knock on his own door. He did not answer, and pretended he was asleep; he closed his eyes and tried to will this monster

68

away. Another knock: silence. Finally the footsteps receded, and when Shaun looked up there was a triangle of color—purple, vermilion, scarlet—poking in under the door. He went over and picked up the small square of paper, blurred and mottled from the rain. He held it up to the window, and it was only then that he discerned the shape of a hastily scrawled heart, and the three words "love, love, love" trapped forever in the purple parchment.

He set the note down on the table and went out—past the sleepy roommate, through the door, down the stairs—into the soft and lovely air of spring. The trees, bare an hour before, had bloomed with small, pale leaves and whitish flowers, and sounds—a dog's bark, a crying child, a drop of water beating off a garbage can lid—hovered in the cool even light. A pretty mother pushed a baby carriage past with a satisfying crunch, and the red bricks of the sidewalk shone in an unusual shade of rust. At the corner the familiar gas station assumed a calm, dignified beauty, the blue neon of its sign held in perfect, luminous balance with the translucent pale blue of sky.

At the corner Shaun turned into the alley beside her house. The backyard was cast in shadow, the grass was very green, the fence's metal latch wonderfully functional. In the week since he had last been there the forsythia bush had faded, displaced by a florid, blooming lilac.

The sliding glass doors were open, and through them drifted the strains of a familiar song which only then did he realize he had missed. He did not enter immediately, but stood for a moment looking in, and then watched as Laura and her roommate came up the stairs laughing, and swept across the room in an effortless succession of revolutions, their arms spread like wings. And when she finally looked out and saw him, it was with a look neither of great joy nor of surprise; instead she reached calmly toward him with a pale, extended hand, as if she had been expecting him for days, and pulled him gently back into her world.

Indian Summer

My grandmother's farm lies off a bend in Route 10, an asphalt ribbon that lies among the hills and towns and farms of southwestern Ohio. The road crosses the highway at Catapult, rises up a slight grade past the steel mill, then winds for two or three miles through woods before giving way to open fields. On a sharp turn to the left, it meets Steuben Road and spills over a small creek, past a pig farm, and then rides the undulating spine of cornfields; it swerves, dips, rises, and there, off to the left, down a red dirt road, her house sits in a lush, low hollow of land. She has recently had the house repainted, the barn cleaned and repointed, the stone wall at the edge of the field restored to the remembered condition of her childhood.

Soon after my grandfather died, several years ago, she bought a horse, but on her first attempt to ride she was thrown off, and their relationship has since been one of mutual respect, and its bounds are clearly understood. Talbot lives in the lower part of the barn, and spends his days in the field below. Twice a day she feeds him, carrying down buckets of water and grain, and in the evening, with the sound of hooves hitting the packed earth, he comes ambling up through the dusk like a heavy ghost and disappears into his stable.

I visited my grandmother there last fall, riding the familiar bus out from the city where I now live. She picked me up at the station, and we drove the few miles back to the house. In the evening, when I went out to walk the dog, she asked me to find a couple of fallen ears of corn for Talbot. "Just look along the edges of the rows," she told me, "where the deer knock them off." There are ninety acres of corn there, all rustling then in the autumn wind, and as I scanned the turned earth in the dying light I was tempted to pull the corn off the stalks instead. But in deference to rural etiquette I resisted, and, in time, I found two ears pressed into the soft red soil under wilting leaves and retraced my steps back toward the yellow light of the house.

In the absence of people, my grandmother has surrounded herself with animals—the horse, the dog, the birds that flock to her, peck birdseed from her hand, and flutter through the trees and surrounding woods. Through years of patronage, she has brought the cat population to something near twenty, and at dinnertime they surround the back door, peering from under bushes or behind the wheels of the parked car. The lawn is marked with the trails of their habitual routes. She tries to find homes for the healthiest, but their expanding numbers oppress her, and it is now a situation without remedy. She knows cats by family and generation—whose grandmother was whose—and follows their comings and goings with a kind of familial love.

"They're really just as different from each other as people are," she tells me as we walk down to the barn. I am carrying a bucket of water and the two ears of corn, husked now, hard and smooth to the touch, their kernels yellow, orange, brown. She unlatches the stable door, we go in, and in the jangled light and shadows I can see her old, dusty saddle, bought secondhand and used only once, hanging from a rusty nail, ancient farm implements leaning in a cobwebbed corner, hay strewn over the floor and piled in bales against the wall. The smell of straw mixes with an underground darkness. I lay the corn in the trough, and Talbot comes shuffling over and, with the sound of marbles being crushed, eats it, his black lips rising and falling over yellow teeth. With a sound that I have never heard before, an almost inaudible sigh, my grandmother startles me, and I look over to where, in the pool of her flashlight, she has come upon a nest of sleeping kittens—a mass of intertwined bodies and pairs of blinking eyes—lying in the hay.

"Isn't that something?" she says softly, as if trying not to wake them. They are blinking to consciousness now, their eyes straining like moths toward the light.

"They're only a few days old, and they're sick, too," she tells me, and it is only then that I notice their eyes are clouded over in a kind of half blindness. They are not so much seeing the light as feeling it. We stand for a moment looking down at them, and then turn and go out. It is a relief, somehow, to be out in the cool, clear air. There is a smell of autumn, of exhaling earth, and in our absence the sky has become filled with stars.

"What a vision of life that was," my grandmother says when we are back in the house, her head slowly shaking in disbelief. "You see, it's confusing. That mother is not one of ours. These people come along the road and leave them off. And then they move into the barn and start making kittens. You'd think it was simple for an old woman to live alone in the middle of nowhere, but not this grandma." Her face clenches and her eyes close in a characteristic prelude to laughter, and her hand reaches up to touch the bridge of her nose, as if to harness, or dampen, her amusement. "No, no," she says. "Not this grandma."

She has lived here all her life, and now wonders what will happen to the farm when she can no longer remain. On each of my visits she asks me advice: whether to let the farmers who lease the land plant a row of peach trees, where to sell a corner parcel in the woods so the Schmeils's son can build a house, whether to let the men cut firewood—questions all suggesting the greater one, What to do with the farm?

I tell her not to sell it, even though her three grand-children love the city and the sea, and show no desire to leave. "You never know," I say. "You never know."

In the last year or so my grandmother has experienced what the doctors call fibrillation and what she says feels like there is a bird trapped in her chest. She spent a week in the hospital because of chest pains, and to everyone's surprise she seemed oddly happy there. The neighbors came to visit, and advised her to get rid of the animals, as if that were the problem with her health. She sees getting rid of the animals as "a step toward getting rid of me." As she told me from the hospital bed, "My idea is that the animals are good for me, but they don't see it that way. They think the animals tire me out. But it's *they* who tire me out." Her face reddened in a wave of withheld laughter.

Still, she feels the encroachment of the natural world—that there is more for her to do than she is able, and that without her resistance the demands of the farm and nature are collapsing back upon her like a breaking wave. She is wary of winter, of carrying those buckets of water and grain over the ice and snow, and of the way the cold makes her heart race.

"I think it will be all right," she says to me on Saturday morning, "as long as I can keep these two feet under me." As we make our way across the lawn in the warm Indian-summer air, strands of hair rise and fall above her in the wind, and she moves with the slow, easy grace of habit, her motions polished like a stone. Her physical being seems to emanate from the earth—an extension of the trees, the yard, the fields—as if the place she loves had returned the favor in beauty.

On Saturday afternoon, with the help of the neighbors, she jump-starts the tractor and begins to mow the lower field. From the yard I can see her moving back and forth along the edge of fallen grass and hear the slow, sonorous growl of the tractor into the late afternoon. It is almost dark when she comes in, her face flushed from the sun. She is pleased she has been able to get so much done, but is tired, and goes to bed early.

As I lie in bed that night the lights of poachers flash

across the ceiling as they scan the empty fields for deer, and I can hear my grandmother and the dog shifting in their beds. My grandmother once told me she thought there were ghosts in the house. "Friendly ones," she said, as if to reassure me. "You know, that light in my room goes on and off, and the cellar door—sometimes I'll leave it closed and the next time I look it will be open. Or maybe I'm just getting old." But as I lie in bed that night I am suddenly conscious of inexplicable sounds, as if the house were somehow speaking, swelling and contracting between its thick stone walls. I realize that in this room over the past one hundred years have slept my parents, my grandparents, my great-grandparents—a slow succession of evolving, overlapping lives. I am a part of all this, I realize—the leading edge of a lineage I barely know.

I fall asleep, but when I wake it is still dark; I can hear my grandmother going down the stairs and the dog behind her, his nails scratching the bare wood floor. I fall back asleep, and this time when I wake it is morning. The moon has become the sun, and broad beams of light slant into the room. Downstairs, there is a place set for me at the table. I tell my grandmother about the sounds.

"Sometimes there are mice in the attic, or the wind blows the shutters," she says.

I tell her I think they were ghosts, but she only laughs. "Oh, no . . ." she says, her voice trailing off.

After church, my grandmother and I and a friend, Mrs. Saunders, drive down to the cemetery, so that they can visit their respective husbands. My grandfather's grave is simple, with his full name carved into the small granite stone, and a tired American flag that the veterans have put out hanging limply by. She shows me the stones of her parents and grandparents—ornate monuments carved and embellished with the vines and leaves and floral structures of another time, their heavy Germanic names contrived to look as if they were spelled out by overlapping sticks in the reddish stone.

We walk over to Mrs. Saunders's husband, who, she shyly explains, was a widower when they married and when he died was buried with his first wife. And so now she does not know where she belongs. To be buried with her husband means to share him with his previous wife, yet she does not want to be buried alone. There is something melancholy in her dilemma, and as we stand in solutionless silence over the grave of Elmer Saunders I am struck by her concern for a time that will not include her, as if this were the last of life's puzzles, the last riddle she was obliged to solve. She looks up at us, as if for an answer, but instead we all three turn, triply stumped, and walk slowly back toward the car.

That afternoon I take a long walk in the fields above the house. At the edge of the woods I cut through a gap in the trees and make my way back along the road. When I reach the junction of Kramer and Steuben, I stop. Steuben slopes gently back toward the farm; Kramer follows a row of listing telephone poles back to Route 10 and, in the other direction, skirts the edge of the field and spills down a long, steep hill into a neighboring valley of farms and horses and handsome stone houses. I remember as a child driving down this road with my grandfather when a flock of chickens suddenly appeared in the road, and as my grandfather braked they squawked and fluttered up in front of the car, scurrying to reach the other side;

this sight induced in my grandfather laughter that did not stop as we drove on past but lingered in him for days, reappearing now and then as a faint glimmer in his eyes. "God, that was comical," he would say, and slowly begin to laugh.

This is the junction where as a child, my grandmother told me, she once met her father when she had been sent to retrieve him from a bout of drinking at the local hotel. After she got to the corner she could see him coming, but when he reached her he did not stop, said nothing, and marched on past her toward the farm. "I never forgave him for that," she told me, her eyes closing and her head shaking in a hurt that is sixty years old.

I love standing at these rural crossroads. The people in passing cars do not know me; the dog does not know why we have stopped. Rows of trees—apple, peach, plum—stand in silent rows and recede through the mist toward the outline of distant hills. The fields of my grandmother's farm stretch away in a kind of optical distortion, as if twisted, bent by time—dipping, then rising to meet the edge of the woods a half mile away. Cars appear on the horizon, shimmer into the middle distance, and then fly past with a sudden rush of wind. I throw pebbles against the sign, watch a flock of geese settle on the neighbor's field, then walk back along the road to the farm.

My grandmother is alone at the kitchen table when I come in. The dog collapses onto the floor, and the clock ticks off the heavy silence of a Sunday afternoon. She asks me if I want a cup of tea, and as she puts on the water she breaks the silence with a sigh. "Well, the kittens are sleeping," she says. It is a minute before I understand.

"You put them to sleep?"

"Down by the spring," she says. "I buried them under the boxwood tree." She sits down in a chair by the window, looking out. "It was peaceful," she adds, but I hear in her voice no sign of consolation.

I picture the landscape she is looking out on, the fields rolling out and away. I want to say something, to disrupt the quiet of her thoughts. "Shall we feed the horse?" I propose.

"Yes," she says, turning to me. "I guess it's about that time. He's getting nervous, just like the rest of us."

She laughs at what she has said and we go out, the dog sprinting out before us to the barn.

Bachelor of Arts

Henry's last term at college, compared to the balmy springs of most graduating seniors, was a cool and rainy fall. Two years before, as an imagined remedy for academic fatigue and as a needed respite from a long, strenuous love affair, he had taken a term off, stumbled aimlessly around Europe for several months, and then gone back to his summer job at a local tennis club, raking clay and laying tapes and repairing dilapidated fences. He returned to college the following fall, but as a consequence of this term-long hiatus the symmetry of his four years was disrupted—transformed into a lopsided three springs and five autumns. As he began his courses the next September, he felt he was reliving part of his past or, like a man cast as himself in his own play, taking an active role in the enactment of his own nostalgia. Added to this were his academic foibles of the previous spring, when for the first time in his life he had failed a course, so that he was now obliged to take five instead of the usual four. With a novel air of gravity surrounding his schooling, and feeling he had outgrown the cloistered world of the dormitory, he moved from his old college room to a large wooden house not far away, sharing his new adult life with a middle-aged lawyer, her carpenter boyfriend, and a young man named Jim, who was trying to break into the music business by producing a radio program entitled "Country Greats in Concert." Henry lived alone on the third floor, and as he lay in bed at night he could hear the melancholy strains of "Country Greats" wafting up the stairs to his room. From his window he could look down onto the tops of the trees and watch as, for no apparent reason, a leaf would suddenly release itself, fall from a motionless branch, and drift down onto the windshield of a parked car, its reflection falling upward through the tinted glass.

By day, he attended his classes with a regularity previously unknown to him—trudging off in the morning with an armful of books, cutting a clean line across the campus, finding a seat in the auditorium and leaning back as the lecture began, recording its "salient points" in his notebook in a small, dutiful script. But as he followed the happy throng of students between classes he noticed that these were people he did not know. In extending his education beyond the projected four years, he had outlived the presence of his peers and come into an unimagined era of strangers. College was something constant, ongoing, he realized, and for all the people he recognized there were countless others coming up behind, usurping them, taking their places in a world of transients. He had lived into a time that no longer included him and was already reaching to embrace the hopeful lives of younger, fresher students.

Now and then he would come upon familiar faces. In Classics of Historical Literature, for example, taught by a booming, bearlike man whose eyes would clamp shut in a kind of rapturous swoon as he recalled, for the thousandth time, an anecdote about one of his heroes, Henry was amused to discover the nape of his first girlfriend, the familiar inclination of her head, three rows down to the right. As the professor marched through the *Decline and Fall of the Roman Empire* and the class transcribed his ramblings in their varied hands, Henry examined the down on the back of her neck, amazed that she, for whom he would once have given a finger in sacrifice, now elicited only a distant wash of fondness which did not lapse into regret. Instead, he felt a faint pity for her new boyfriend, in whom, when he met him once after class, he detected the same glint of hopelessness he had once felt in himself.

One day when he sat beside her, he was amused by her industry, the ceaseless stream of notes that flowed from her purple pen, the way she frantically flopped the notebook pages over in midsentence, as if in fear of missing a single word. A beam of sunlight fell through the window and bathed them both in a warm, autumnal glow; he leaned toward her and tried to inhale the fragrance that had once tormented him—it was there, but it did not draw him nearer. He was touched by the trappings of her new life: new haircut and shoes, unfamiliar clothes, the sky-blue bicycle she hurriedly unlocked and on which, like a man in a silent movie, she teetered away across the campus.

After class Henry went out through the iron gates, across the avenue, and turned in to his favorite Chinese restaurant, and there, with one of his schoolbooks for company, he ordered a bowl of soup and fried rice and, as he ate, listened to the quarrel of two young lovers and the exchange of an old man and his grandson debating the contents of an egg roll. As he walked home he could hear the sound of "Country Greats" a block away, and on his way upstairs he looked in as Jim and a friend played and replayed a single song. "Hey, Henry!" Jim said suddenly, noticing him in the doorway. "How's school?"

That night, when Henry finished all his studying and found that the few friends he called weren't home, he went out by himself, strolling in and out of bookstores, pausing for a cup of coffee, looking into bars for someone he knew, and then drifted back to his room. On this and other walks, he discovered the first peculiar lesson of adulthood: its strange, inescapable loneliness.

His courses went well. His method of studying was foolproof, and for the first time he felt the yeomanlike satisfaction of diligence. He was amused by simple things—the interrelatedness of his subjects. In the week he was studying Gibbon's *The Decline and Fall of the Roman Empire*, for example, he learned in Anthropology 99 that gibbons, tree-swinging apes, were prone to humanlike error: a random sampling of skeletons from a certain Asian jungle revealed that a high percentage of the gibbons had at one time or another suffered broken bones, presumably caused by their airborne miscalculations—a branch missed and a long, bloodcurdling scream as they fell like stones, carrying fistfuls of shredded leaves to the jungle floor. The two teachers of this course seemed to mimic the characteristics of two distinct varieties of primates: the one short, rotund, and stout, with a head of auburn hair, distant kin of the chimpanzee, orangutan, gorilla, and other slow-moving apes; the other light-limbed, delicate, bifocaled, resembling the nimble, arboreal vegetarians—lemurs, spider monkeys—who spent their entire simian lives, Henry read, in the "verdant, airy world of the forest canopy."

The teacher of Russian 102 was an affable, limping Russian with a cane. The class, the last of Henry's morning, was held at eleven in a cozy, coffin-shaped room in Bartram, in the middle of the campus. The seats were upholstered and, in conjunction with the sonorous voice of Professor Slokov, induced in Henry a half-reclining position of daydreaming contemplation.

The autumn gave way to a succession of gray, rainy, wintry days, and from his seat he could look out and up at the falling leaves as they were swept past the window, only to tumble, he imagined, to a resting place under a bush or pasted to the sole of a nervous freshman's plodding shoe. In time, Henry's attention turned toward a young woman he distantly knew, sitting a few rows in front of him and wearing glasses. His interest in Russian literature was slowly displaced, and each successive class witnessed his steady migration across the room, the gap between his seat and hers diminishing until there was only one seat between them, and then, on the next day, no seat at all. They began to have small pre- and postclass conversations, and during class, as they leaned back in their chairs, they would exchange whispered imitations of Professor Slokov's Russian accent. Sandra was a Russian major and, she later told him, part Russian, and so she would point out the connotations of certain words, the nuances of phrases. But mostly they just sat in a kind of happy silence, Henry pleased there was someone to share this sleepy interim of the day with. One morning he wore a short-sleeved shirt and the back of his arm lightly touched against the back of hers, and to his surprise she didn't move her arm away. He closed his eyes and listened to the sound of rain as drops began to pelt against the window, and felt, in this faint exchange of heat, a distant signal of acquiescence.

Several days later he ran into her at the athletic fields during halftime of an intramural soccer game he was playing in. She was wearing high leather boots, a plaid skirt, a low-cut sweater almost the color of her own pale skin. As they stood together, talking, the light mist that had begun to fall gathered like beads in her hair, and the smell of grass and mud mingled with the distant scent of her perfume.

"So how've you been?" he said, tossing a muddy soccer ball up into the air and catching it.

"Oh, all right," she answered, staring distractedly away across the fields. "A little horny, I guess."

He was so surprised by this simple self-observation— by this word he had never heard spoken by a woman before—that he laughed. "Well, you can't have everything," he said, intending to make *her* laugh, though she didn't. Instead, a shrill whistle blew, he said good-bye and sprinted back into the game.

A few weeks later he called her impulsively on a cold,

rainy night, and they met at a small bar near his house. Outside of class, she seemed different, transformed. She wore the same low-cut sweater and had exchanged her glasses for contacts. They spoke of inconsequential things—Professor Slokov, the thesis she was writing on Pushkin, the six months she had once spent in Russia. As they talked Henry gathered she had a boyfriend somewhere, hidden away in another city. He soon learned that the boyfriend was French, that the city was Paris, and that she had met him the year before, when he was a graduate student in medieval history. It also became apparent that her happiness hinged on the tenor of her weekly phone conversations with him, and that in his absence she suffered a certain sense of displacement, dislocation—as if the world to which she had previously belonged no longer existed. Like Henry, she was living out her last college year more from necessity than desire.

On the way home he invited her into his house, but she begged off. "Some other time," she said, and then, as if in consolation, she suddenly, passionately kissed him, her hand landing like a wild bird on the curve of his hip, his cupping the hollow of her back. "See you in class," she said, finally, and kissed him again.

Henry went up to his room with a sudden sense of good fortune and a peculiar gratitude for being alone. He did not immediately go to sleep but sat up in the darkness looking out the window and listening to the sound of leaves falling through the windless air.

In class, they continued to sit together, to whisper and talk, and did so with the pleasant sensation of a shared secret. In the chaste light of Russian literature her beauty seemed to take on softer, richer tones. They met again at a small subterranean bistro near her dorm and had several drinks—he beer, she seven and seven.

"So how's your boyfriend?" Henry asked.

"Oh, not too good," she said, looking down at the table, tapping together two coins with two pale fingers. "I talked to him last night and he told me he wasn't coming for Christmas, and so I got mad and told him I was going there, and then he started talking about his mother, how there wasn't any room in the house, blah, blah, blah . . ."

"Well, he'll call back," Henry weakly offered.

"Yeah, well, he's supposed to call tomorrow," she said. "It's just a pain." With that, the conversation shifted; their mutual acceptance of this boyfriend seemed to offer safety somehow—a necessary, unspoken boundary.

On the way back he repeated his previous invitation, she accepted, and he led her up the dark diagonal of the stairway to his room. They knelt on the bed by the window looking out on the street below, and watched as a small dog tugged its master from hedge to hydrant and a man on a bicycle glided by beneath them. While trying to see a cat creeping along the top of a picket fence, they touched shoulders and then, with the sure, inevitable pull of gravity, they resumed the kiss with which they had parted the last time he had seen her. But as Henry watched her face in the muted darkness of the room, her eyes closed like two translucent shells, it suddenly came to him, with the abrupt clarity of a dream, that her expression was no longer her own but, rather, that of someone he had never met before. She seemed distant, alone—as if what she was thinking could not be shared. He wanted to say something to break the silence, but then realized he didn't know her well enough to know what to say. He was relieved when she kissed him good-bye and went quietly from his room; he listened as her footsteps receded down the stairs and the front door thumped shut behind her.

The next day, she was not in class; the day after, he was not; and then, like little lights going out, each of Henry's classes ended to a faint smattering of student applause. Professor Slokov gave a little bow, and the term was suddenly over.

In the week before final exams Henry methodically reviewed for each of his courses, finished a paper on "The Idiosyncrasies of Primate Evolution," and otherwise tied up the loose ends of his formal education. Even if he failed his exams, he calculated, he would still pass and graduate. He knew most of his grades already: A, A-, B, B-, C. The C was in Russian.

He ran into Sandra one afternoon as he was walking slowly home from a bout with sleep at the library and she tripped into his path down the steps of Fowler.

"What are your plans?" she asked him, but he didn't really know.

"I might go skiing for a while," he said, "and then I should find a job—gardening, maybe."

Although it was December, the weather was warm and Henry was dressed in a worn-out sports jacket, in the standard style of the college. While he stood talking with her in the dying light, the wind whipped up the scents of the decaying autumn, and she lightly held, tugging and releasing by turns, the tired cloth of his lapel. He was moved more by this small gesture than he had been by her visit to his room and as she fastened and unfastened a single button on his coat he was also moved by the sudden, impromptu conjunction of impressions, and by a premonition that these would be the last things he would remember of college: the faint fragrances of leaves, wet wool, perfume; the wonderful hovering sensation of enclosing dusk. As he looked up toward the lit windows of the college rooms he felt safe, protected from the world that would soon claim him, and, if only for the moment, loved.

Agawam

The town where I grew up shares its name with that of the river that runs through it, and with the tribe of Indians that once called this part of Massachusetts their home. The river arrives from the west, having wound its way through woods and fields and small New England towns, flowing under bridges and over rocks and fallen trees, through turns and bends and under the ropes from which boys swing in summer; past the canoe landing, the brick factory, and over a waterfall, arriving in town with a soft, insistent babble. It then passes behind the banks and barber shops and stores, under another bridge, around another bend where it meets and merges with the salt water that rises and falls from the sea.

And as the river flows on, the town just sits, observing a tidal world of its own—the ebb and flow of night and day, the weeks, the months, the seasons—the gentle, ceaseless flux of the generations. Although I have lived away, in other places, since I was sixteen, the town has remained my emotional center, the place to which I return with the sure, inevitable motion of gravity, like a falling stone.

My favorite means of coming back has always been by train. The plane is too dangerous and fast, a car too confining and slow; but the train moves along at the pace of passing thoughts, carrying me on the back of its vast, irresistible mass, as light as a feather. Our journey is marked by the steady click of couplings and the welcome recession of the city—the backyards of Brooklyn and Queens giving way to the vacant lots and abandoned buildings of the Bronx, and then to the houses and golf courses of the suburbs. By now I know it almost all by heart—a familiar grove of trees, a deserted beach, an empty field opening up into a sudden, breathless bay of blue. There are minor cities and their landmarks: decaying battleships in a turgid harbor, the scrawled message "I love Irene" on a crumbling wall, the candy factory with its enormous, comical rows of lifesavers tipped on end in a jaunty row. And there is the place where the train inexplicably pauses, catching its breath, and the beautiful elm tree that grows there along a barren factory wall. There are familiar stretches of marsh and field, a remembered house on a peninsula of stone, frozen ponds etched with the skate marks of now absent children. After a nap, a hundred pages of a book, a fleeting dream oddly syncopated with the flickering visions outside, another city appears: tired triple-deckers, laundry swaying stiffly in the wind, black children, and then white, playing in squalid yards. The train creaks over archaic bridges and pilings rotting in oily canals, then hisses, lurches, stops, and a man in a blue uniform calls out that we have arrived. "Last stop. Everybody out!" There is the slow procession up the isle, the crushed scents of our fellow passengers, the cool, gray air of another city.

And soon I am on another train, older and more rickety than the first. The windows are plastic and scratched, but the landscape outside is my own, and the chant of the conductor, barking out a familiar litany of towns, is a song I have known since childhood. Outside there are the same forgotten factories and scrap metal yards, and then woods and fields as the city turns into a succession of diminishing towns.

"Agawam, Agawam!" the conductor finally shouts, and everyone, even the drunken man who has overslept his stop, shuffles down the aisle and spills into town. Town.

No one has guessed or anticipated my arrival, and so I walk—past the bank, the movie theater, the barber shop, and the drugstore with its wavering neon sign that says "Prescriptions." It is spring, and the sidewalk is bleached by sand and salt, like an old, faded photograph. I pass the faces of people I used to know, the library, the Odd Fellows hall, and walk across the playing fields between the two brick buildings where I once attended school. I cross the street and then the bridge that spans the river on which boats, like ducks, have just swung with the tide, and follow the road that leads the last mile to the house. When I am almost there I cut through a gap in the bushes, climb a small knoll at the edge of the field and whistle. I stop, whistle again, and across the field a speck appears, stops, and then bounds toward me, sprinting across the matted grass, ears flapping, teeth showing, his four feet consuming the space between us; he circles around and past me and finally stops, and I bend to pet his happy, panting head as together we walk back across the field to the house.

But the dog of this picture is no more, having subsided into the earth and the memories of those who knew him, and other aspects of this journey, itself a composite of many I have made, have been rendered obsolete: a block of buildings on Main Street has since burned down, replaced by a discreet, miniature mall; the movie theater has been closed for lack of business and then razed, transformed into a parking lot for the bank; and strangest of all, someone has turned my old elementary school into "15 Green Street," a parody of a castle with clipped hedges and glittering chandeliers—the dusty classrooms where I learned to read and write reincarnated as condominiums. Now there is another baby boom, and there is talk of building a new elementary school to replace the one they sold to the developers. Downtown the cars seem fancier than when I was growing up, and the stores seem to be catering to people who have more money than they know what to do with. And although I have nothing against people in headlong pursuit of their careers, I have come to associate them with the rather peculiar changes in town. As a result I have distanced myself, abandoning what I know and love rather than watch it evolve into something I don't know or understand.

As a child, I was resistant both to change, and to leaving home. My several months away at summer camp were extremely unhappy ones—long, rainy days drifting through a wooded world seen in duplicate, defracted by

the prism of my tears. And when I was sent away to prep
school at age fourteen, I lasted only a month until, after
daily, desperate telephone calls, I convinced my parents
of my genuine unhappiness and was allowed to return
home. Even later, during college, my several trips abroad
ended with a triumphant, euphoric return, and as I sat
on the plane, or train, it was with a vast, unutterable sense
of relief, or gratitude, for getting home alive. After I grad-
uated and moved to the city, I continued to return to the
town, to the house where I grew up, and remained there
for weeks, months, while I mustered enough courage to
return to the "real world."

It was during one of these prolonged visits home, my
life suspended between apartments, girlfriends, jobs,
wavering between the life I was living and the life I felt
I should be living somewhere else, that I came upon the
idea of building a one-room house for myself in the
woods. What gave me this idea I am not exactly sure: a
combination of too much energy, and an acute need to
do something without knowing, exactly, what it was.
When finished, I imagined this house would afford a kind
of safety net, a functional symbol, a place to which,
should all else fail in the real world, I could always return.
With these foggy notions swirling in my mind I began to
scout around my mother's property in search of a place
to build on, and soon found one in a deep thicket of
woods halfway between the marsh and the field. I received rather vague, disbelieving permission from my
mother, and returned to the site one afternoon with a
shovel and pick ax and began thrashing through the undergrowth, clearing the topsoil in a rough rectangle of
land where, I imagined, the little house would sit. A few

days later I dug holes for the foundations, filled them with rocks and cinder blocks, and began to look around for used lumber. I found some old barn boards in the cellar, some heavy posts in the barn, but my greatest find of all was an enormous beam, eight by twelve and seventeen feet long, that had washed up on the marsh and lay there like a beached whale, wet and salty from daily washings of the tides. With a long pole as a lever I managed to raise the beam a few inches off the marsh to dry out, and several days later, using boards and roller in the style of the ancient Egyptians, I managed to coax it down the narrow winding path to the site. I then raised it up onto the cinder blocks, made it level with a section of telephone pole, and it thus became the structural center, the backbone of the little house.

What wood I couldn't find around the house I bought from eighty-year-old Mr. Daniels, who ran a small sawmill in a neighboring town.

"What can I do for you?" he would ask, stepping out of his delapidated house, wiping bread crumbs from his mouth, two small dogs yapping at his heels. We would walk together to an old shed, select some beams and boards from a pile, and load them into the back of my mother's car.

"Well, come back when you need some more," he offered, wiping the sweat from his face with an old handkerchief, "I'll be here—either here, or out back, under a pile of wood." He laughed at his own joke, the thought of his own demise, his yellow teeth bared to the hard light of the sun.

The greatest boon to my scavenging came, oddly, when developers began to dismantle my old elementary school and turn it into condominiums. One by one the old floorboards, bent and gnarled and giving off the smell of shellac, came flying out the window and landed in a tangled nest on my old playground. I received permission from a distracted Polish foreman, drove up in the car and shuttled these boards back to the house.

I soon moved back to the city, and began to pursue something resembling a career, but on my visits home I continued to build, and the little house slowly began to ascend. I lay in the underbeams—"joists"—nailed on pine boards for the floor and, using posts and beams held together with oak pegs I had carved, I constructed a frame in the style of old barns. In the cellar I found some old casement windows, built frames for them in the walls, and put in a small blue door my mother had pilfered from someone's trash. I cut rafters, nailed them to the ridgepole, and then sheathed the whole house with barn boards bought from Mr. Daniels. I tarpapered the roof, wheeled out an old wood stove, ran a stovepipe up the wall, and soon had the illusion, if not the fact, of warmth. And though there were still cracks in the walls and the floor where the wind whistled through, the little house was finished, after two years of sporadic though persistent labor.

Though my life has since come together, somewhat, and I have settled in another city, when I do return it is with the same sense of excitement, of falling back through time, of returning to the place where, by some unspoken right of birth, I still belong. I love seeing the town, the road, the house, the three dogs that my mother, as if in replacement of her children, now takes care of. But I no longer sleep in my old bed in my old room, finding the air there too constricting, rich, filled with the shades and shadows of some other, difficult time.

At Christmas, when the house fills with family and friends, I feel happy, though heavy, and everything seems imbued with some elusive double meaning—childhood anxieties distilled as adult angst. I wander through the rooms like a lost ghost, and then go out across the lawn to the path at the edge of the woods. All is quiet and filled with the scent of pine. A crow swoops down from a branch, settles on another, caws once, and flops away. The path veers through two thin maples, turns up a rise, and there it is, sitting on a small knoll in the trees. The walls are bare wood, still damp from the rain, and the door opens easily, admitting me to a small, cool space with a rough wood floor and a single, awaiting chair. In one corner there is a wood stove, and through two skylights falls a soft, even light. There is still more to be done, but at the moment I have little time for these improvements. My stay is too short, and I am happy for the house to be as it is, shedding the rain and the snow, absorbing the nights and the days and the seasons, collecting the leaves and pine needles that settle on its roof, looking more and more like it has always been there.

I light a small fire and sit, listening to the voices of clammers who haunt the marsh at low tide. Through the windows I can see the creek, and the field, and through the skylights I watch shifting patterns in the sky. My family has recently taken more interest in this part of the woods, and I can hear someone crunching through the underbrush, sawing branches, domesticating nature. I think I know how the Indians, the Agawams, must have felt when they first heard the ominous sounds of the white man.

But as Americans we are encouraged, always, to move on, to go away to someplace better, or different, as if to remain in the place where we are from is symptomatic of some greater, unspoken failure. And on my visits home I soon grow restless. The air is too thick, and my vision grows cloudy; I feel I am moving too slowly, like a man at the bottom of the sea. I wonder what my friends are doing in the place where I now live, and I wonder what I am doing in the place where I was once a boy. Strangely, the closer the little house had come to completion, the more obscure had become its function, as if in the very act of construction I had undergone some sort of transformation, a catharsis at once preserving the past and outliving it. All that time I was working alone in the woods, sawing boards and banging nails and wrestling with enormous beams, something was silently changing, and when I finished and looked up, it was only to discover that the earth had shifted beneath me, and the place to which I had always returned now pressed me gently away.

Winter

Through the cool glass of the window Robert looked down and across the street to where a small child dressed in blue, a girl, he thought, was playing. She was pushing a swing back and forth to a man in a black overcoat, and now and then she would break into a sudden, wobbly run, sending a flock of pigeons fluttering up into the branches above. The view was otherwise colorless, shades of red brick and gray and brown, and reminded him of a faded photograph, or a half-remembered scene from his own childhood. He could dimly hear the sounds of children playing on the street below, and there was something in their voices that reminded him of people on a beach in summer. Along the sidewalk an old woman walked her dog, and two teenaged girls in cheap fur coats and tight pants languidly strolled. Even from a distance, he was moved by their beauty, youth, and the taut suggestive sway of adolescence. He watched them until they were out of sight, and when he looked back at the playground the man and child were gone, and one by one the pigeons swooped down onto the pavement, fluttering onto their own shadows.

The windowpane was cold, the room was cool, the teapot on his desk was lukewarm. His room was white and square and filled with objects that all reminded him of her, relics of their newly dissolved relationship. He could neither look at them nor take them down and so he pulled on his coat and hat instead and went out into the gray streets of the city.

It was Saturday, shopping day: women shuffled along the pavement with cartloads of laundry, parents and their children walked hand in hand toward the park, a tired brown football floated across the street, buoyed up by the shouts of teenaged boys. A single dog bark rose in the thin air, heightened by the winter stillness which, in his memory of things, generally preceded snow. Higher still, flecks of blue and white and silver—pigeons—wheeled above the chimney pots and rooftops of Brooklyn.

In the park the earth was frozen and bare, the sidewalk bleached by sand and salt spread after the season's first storm. Across the street an abandoned movie theatre, the Rialto, was boarded up and covered with graffiti, its once grand alcove a wind trap for urban flotsam—old bus tickets and paper cups and fallen leaves—swept into a neat, triangular pile under an abandoned ticket kiosk.

The windows of the local elementary school were decorated with pumpkins and turkeys and enormous snowflakes, and the stores were filled with tawdry merchandise on post-Christmas sale. As he walked he wondered how he, a country boy from New England, had come to find himself here, in the middle of Brooklyn. The incongruity of it all hit him with a familiar weight, heightened to a painful clarity by the knowledge that his initial reason for moving to the city had ceased to be. As of two days before, she had ceased to be his lover.

"You're like a brother to me," she had offered by way of explanation, but this had maddened, then saddened him, suggesting a kind of finity, a relegation to the platonic he could not absorb. Ever since her call he had felt as though he was in a peculiar dream: while his body performed, by habit, all the necessary functions of existence, his mind worked its own swirling course, trying to assimilate this incongruous fact to some deeper layer of his understanding.

"I don't want to be your brother," he had said angrily. "I don't want to be your friend. I have friends coming out of my ears, and where are they all now?" It was true. Since Sarah had left the city three months before, their mutual friends had receded, and in their absence he too had withdrawn, collapsed into a shell of solitude from which he neither wanted, nor knew how, to escape.

He turned into a corner newsstand, bought a paper, and then stepped into a small luncheonette across the street. Above the door a large neon sign spelled "Donuts," in script, and inside it was done up in a fifties version of the vogue: pink plastic, a tiled floor, drooping plants. Though neat and clean it always seemed to be almost empty—a few policemen, low-level real estate entrepreneurs huddled over an impending deal, the plump, pretty high-school girls with pink legs and plaid skirts sipping milk shakes. And always there were a few old men who

came to escape their steam-heated rooms and sat alone
at the booths, held in clouds of their own cigarettes.

The restaurant must have been cheerful once, but
there was something in the way everything looked dated,
in the way the sunlight fell through the windows in the
late afternoon, the way the cars drifted past outside, that
heightened the sense of stasis, of passing time, and the
emptiness of the huddled lives within. The coffee was
forever steaming in its pots, and the donuts patiently
waited to be eaten, becoming ever staler in their rows.
Oddly, Robert did find it cheerful here, or at least more
so than his own room. Here, at least, loneliness was the
communal element, the collective medium in which
everyone lived and thrived.

He admired the waitresses for their persistent, lingering
beauty, their gritty urban toughness; among them was a
woman with brown hair and a shapely figure who treated
Henry with a reassuring familiarity, remembered that he
liked his eggs scrambled, and often stood within his view,
hip cocked, cigarette in hand, staring out through the
window as if waiting for her old high-school sweetheart
to drive up and take her away.

"Coffee, hon?" she now said, pouring it into his cup
before he had a chance to answer.

"Yes, please." He tried to impart to his voice a genuine
sense of gratitude, and then watched her as she walked
away.

The paper read, the two cups of coffee drank, Robert
paid and stepped out into the street, dropping the paper
into the trash and then heading into the park. People
drifted along the paths, joggers puffed along the roadway,

and on a distant field two teams swept back and forth across the yellow grass like fallen leaves.

The almost bare branches swayed slightly in a faint, tremulous wind.

And though he had always found a kind of solace in the park, a respite from solitude, now the stillness seemed to crowd him, to press him deeper into himself. He had seen Sarah only twice since she had left the city, spoken with her only occasionally on the phone, but in his mind they had remained together, and he had hoped that their relationship would revive and continue. For the first time, he had begun to imagine her as his wife.

"Call me later, if you want to," she had said at the end of their last conversation, and though he had resolved not to, this resolution now fell away, and it came as a surprise to realize that he could still call her, talk to her. He stopped and retraced his steps back across the field. By the time he reached the playground he was almost running; he leapt over the stone wall, crossed the street, fumbled with his keys, and then silently ascended, two steps at a time, to his room. He could hear his own heart beating as he dialed. The phone rang, once, twice . . .

"Is Sarah there?" he asked, sounding to himself like a trespasser, as if it was no longer his province to ask.

The voice did not answer, but he could hear footsteps receding, and then others approach.

"Hello," Sarah said softly. It was a relief, to hear her voice.

"Hello."

"Hi, how are you?" she said slowly, distending the words into long, empathetic notes, like the song of a bird.

"Fine," Robert said, and then corrected himself. "Terrible, I mean."

"Why? What's the matter?"

"What do you think?—everything. Nothing makes sense to me."

"Like what?"

"Like everything. Anything." He could feel a flood of words rising up from somewhere near the center of his body, spilling out of his mouth like water over a dam. "Me, you—the fact that we just broke up. The fact that I live alone in the middle of this God forsaken place. I don't even know how I got here. I followed you here and then you decided to leave and now there's nothing left. I might as well be on the moon. No one calls. No one writes. This is the first time I've spoken all day," he said, surprised himself at the realization.

"Why don't you call your friends?"

"They've all gone. They've all left. Everyone's busy in this city. You have to call them a month in advance just to meet for a coffee. And then you call me and tell me we're not together. I don't understand it. I'm upset," he said, "as you may have noticed."

"I can tell you are. But what can I do to help you?"

"You can't. Don't you see? You can't help me anymore. That's what you've given up. If I want consolation I have to find it somewhere else. It's like shooting someone in the foot and then offering them a pair of crutches. It doesn't work that way."

In the silence that followed Robert felt his whole body tingling as if he was receiving a mild electrical shock, and when he looked down at his hand his fingers involuntarily contracted, like slowly closing claws. Why had he called?

"I love you." He said it almost in a whisper, humbled by the words so seldom spoken when they were together.

"I know you do. That's why it's hard. I love you too."

"Then what are we breaking up for?"

He was clutching the receiver so tightly his fingers hurt, and his whole body was huddled over the phone, as if he were trying to make himself small enough to climb in. The stillness seemed to gather around him, the silence given texture only by the dull hiss of the radiator and by the sound of cars passing on the street outside.

"Well, I guess you see it differently," she said finally.

"Why, how do you see it? You just break up and that's it? Why aren't you upset?"

"I am upset, but it's been a long time, Robert. I haven't seen you in months. I've already done my mourning."

"I know all that, but I've still thought of you as my girlfriend. We were still 'together.'"

"It wasn't working. You know that. We weren't helping each other."

"And lately . . . you're the only person I ever thought I could marry . . ." As he said it his voice trailed off, as if he were afraid she might actually hear him.

"Well, thank you. That means a lot to me, Robert."

And as if that was what he meant to say all along, he could feel his anxiety slowly dissipate, like air slowly leaking out of a balloon. "I just can't stand to think it's over."

"Well, don't think of it that way, then. That's high-school stuff. Things aren't working out right now. And rather than drag it through the mud it's better to separate for now, and maybe later things will work out. Maybe not. And in a way it doesn't matter. My feelings for you haven't changed. It's just the form they've taken that's changed."

Although he had always admired her pragmatic view of the world, he had never found much solace in her calm acceptance of things. And though he did not entirely follow the logic of her argument, he found it soothing nonetheless, a balm to whatever it was that ailed him. "I just can't stand to think it's over," he repeated.

"So don't think of it that way. But Robert, I should go now. Some people are waiting for me. I'll be home later tonight if you want to talk some more. Are you alright?"

"Yeah. So why don't you call me sometime?"

"I will. But I have to go right now. I'm sorry, but call me later if you want. And take care of yourself."

"I will."

"O.K."

"Bye."

"Bye."

"Bye." With each repetition the word grew fainter, replaced at last by the dull buzz of the dial tone. When he hung up, he was almost surprised to find that nothing in the room, in his life, had changed: there was the same dusty plant, the same bicycle with two flat tires. Winter's early darkness pressed against the window, and through the gloom he could see people moving on the street outside, and hear the muffled din of the rush hour traffic. He quickly stood up and went out for the walk he had never finished.

Outside the sky was darker still. The air was colder, and as he walked he felt on his face a spark, then another, and another, and he looked up to where, against the bare black branches of the trees, he could see the faint trails of falling snow. Snow! The very idea came as a surprise. Snow gathered on his coat and hat and arms, and out in the street it formed trails in the wake of passing cars. There was something in the way the air had grown colder, in the way the wind had picked up, in the way the flakes rose and fell in the streetlights, that suggested it was a real storm.

He turned into the park, and as he did the sounds of traffic and honking horns fell away almost immediately replaced by a faint, nearly inaudible hush. The light of day was gradually displaced, as if the shades of sky and earth had reversed themselves, and when he reached the edge of the field he turned into the woods and followed a path as it wound down through the trees alongside a frozen stream, passed over a small bridge, and opened up onto a small clearing in the trees. A row of lamp-posts—each illuminating a perfect, cascading bell of white—skirted the edge of the woods, and an old-fashioned bandstand sat in a grove of poplar trees, waiting for spring. Picnic tables stood around in a haphazard cluster, and on one of them Robert lay down on his back in the snow, letting the flakes settle around him, on him, adding him to the landscape of white.

When he first met her she had been a religion major, doing her thesis on Tibetan Buddhism, and that first spring she used to wear a small velvet hat, and her cheeks were always flushed by the soft light of the sun, or perhaps some mysterious, internal glow. "Change," she had once said, "is the only constant in the universe. It's the only thing you can count on. If you fight it, you're bound to be miserable." He could picture the sad, enigmatic smile that had come onto her face, the way the palms of her hands turned slowly upward like those statues of Buddha.

He continued to lie perfectly still, listening to the wind in the trees, the faint hiss of the snow, the distant thumping of his own heart. What if the snow were so heavy he could not move, just lie there as it gathered, the cold slowly seeping into his clothes, his skin, until it finally reached the soft, warm center of his body? He had read somewhere that freezing was among the pleasanter deaths, one's body being consumed, in the end, by a strange and wonderful sense of well-being. And as he lay the snowflakes continued to settle on him, around him, and the cold had begun to work its way down toward a place from which only the warm light of spring would be able to press it out.

And as if this realization induced in his body an involuntary shudder, a spark, a final impulse toward self-preservation, he sat up and looked around him—off to where, in the shadow of the trees, there was someone moving—a woman, and near her a large, lumbering dog bounding along through the snow. He quickly brushed the snow from his coat and hat and arms and watched them approach. As he stood he tried to somehow project an aura of goodwill, so she would not be frightened when she saw him. But the dog saw him first, bounded over, around him, sniffed his outstretched hand and then ran away.

"Roger, Roger! Roger, come here!" the woman shouted, and the big dog ran to her, and then back to him, as if pulling them together by an invisible string.

"Roger, stop it!" she shouted again.

"That's all right, I like dogs," He reached out to touch Roger's panting head.

"It's nice out, isn't it?" he offered and looked up at the woman's face. She was wearing a white hat and a coat with a matching fringe of fur, and she had a kind of seasoned, city toughness.

"Bee-u-tiful!" the woman said, twirling around in the snow.

"Is it supposed to keep snowing?"

"I don't know. I hope it snows forever."

He wanted to say something else, to keep the conversation alive, but what? In the pale, reflected light he could see that she was young and, if not exactly beautiful, pretty in a subtle, knowing way.

"Aren't you afraid of being out in the park late at night?" he asked.

"Why? Are you going to mug me?" she asked, and then laughed at the thought of it. "No. If anyone bothers me Roger will bite their head off. Won't you Roger? Besides, it's snowing. Muggers don't come out in the snow." This, too, made her laugh, and she bent down to hug the happy, panting dog. There was something endearing in the gesture, as if she were somehow imparting trust and affection, to him.

"Well, have a nice night," she said. She stood up, and started down the path. "Come on Roger, come on boy!" She walked backward, clapping to him, turning and breaking into a tripping, unathletic gait.

"You too," Robert called after her, and then watched as she moved down the path disappearing into white. In her absense, he continued to stand perfectly still, listening, watching the footsteps she had left as they were slowly softened, buried, and at last became only rounded hollows in which pale shadows lay.

And as if this woman and her dog had provided some sort of clue, a calm peace finally came over him, descended from nowhere, as if he, too, had finally become a part of all that surrounded him—added to the storm. He was grateful she had stopped, grateful she had not been afraid, grateful she was willing to talk with him. He turned and walked slowly across the field into a part of the park where he had never been. In the distance, the pine trees looked like a scene from a Japanese landscape. He loved the snow, he realized, because it brought with it change, lovely and immediate and unasked for, and for a time concealed the imperfections of this world.

The End of the Reign

M y father left home, after twenty-odd years of marriage, when I was seventeen. It was early June, and spring had just turned into summer, and I spent the day after he told us on the parking lot of the beach where I then worked, dazed as much by the sudden summer heat, the sunlight bouncing off chrome, as by the unimaginable change that had abruptly arrived in my world. That summer I had trouble sleeping, and would lie awake at night conscious of every sound, knowing that I was the last line of defense, and that in the event of burglary it would be left to me to leap down the stairs swinging a golf club or else to throttle the intruder with my bare hands. I kept my job at the beach and tempered my sorrow in a pale, doomed romance with a girl several years my junior. At night, we would drive to the beach parking lot and sit in the shimmering darkness, our ardor kept in check by my ineptitude, her youth, and the bright lights of a police car which occasionally broke into our steamy domain. An inexplicable sadness crept into our meetings, and the romance came to a sudden end one evening as we drove along a lonely country road and, while trying to find a station on the radio, I inadvertently veered to the right and looked up in time to see the car surreally blundering through a row of cement posts and into the woods, plowing over small trees and undergrowth, until we finally met an unmoving maple, which our front bumper instantly embraced. We got out to examine the smoking hulk while the radio continued to play the melancholy song that, at the instant before contact, I had accidentally found. We met several times after that, but this shared calamity somehow stood as the final punctuation of our relationship, and soon thereafter the summer was over.

Several years before, my family had moved to a big white clapboard house on the outskirts of town. The property included on its seven acres of marsh, woods, and field a tired old barn and a small white cottage, which we rented out to a bearded, young musician. In the wake of my father's departure, and with my own impending exodus to college, my mother, made practical by necessity and eager to escape the empty spaces that had suddenly opened up around her, decided to rent the big house and move into the cottage across the way. On a warm, wet autumnal day at the end of August my two sisters, Lea and Susan, and I helped her move our worldly possessions across the driveway, from one house to the other. In bare feet we carried chairs and mattresses and boxes through wind and driving rain, over the leaves and sticks and branches knocked off the trees by a sudden autumn storm. My mother's hair was frazzled from the rain and her exertions. When everything was out she swept through the empty rooms of the big house and mopped all the floors and the move was complete.

The change was welcome. The kitchen of the little house had once been a greenhouse, and its many windowpanes looked out through a grove of pine trees and larches to the barn. Birds came to feed in the yard, fluttering through the branches or pecking across the grass, and our dog and two cats would sit or sleep on the flagstone patio or drift across the lawn like grazing sheep. At all times of day sunlight fell through the branches of the trees and came through the windows, settling in shifting, dappled patterns on the floor of the little house. In its few small rooms everything seemed simplified, compact, and the sudden reduction of space came as a relief rather than a hardship. On the weekends that fall, after taking the train out from college, I'd play tennis with an elderly neighbor on our underused clay court and go on long walks with the dog, Max, over the bridge and then out along the road to the marsh. I slept in the attic of the little house, in a tent-shaped room that resembled the cabin of a ship. Its walls were old oiled wood, and its one large screened window looked out through the pines to the field, and in autumn, the room filled with the scent of apples, slowly decomposing on the ground below.

The structure of our family had not loosened in my father's absence—only shifted, rearranged. When my sister Lea was first married a couple of years before, her husband, Michael Farnsworth—reduced to Farnsworth in his absence—was reluctant to spend time at our house, but when my father left and we moved into the cottage he was eager to visit, and on Sundays he and my sister would appear in their battered gray Toyota, park in the circular drive, and come up the yard to the house.

"Good morning, Peter," my sister would shout up the lawn to me.

"Good morning," I would say, stepping wearily from the kitchen in my stocking feet, kissing my sister and shaking Farnsworth's hand.

"Well, good morning, sir," he would say, suppressing a laugh and then looking away across the scruffy lawn, as if in search of something he had lost.

He was a slight, oddly formal man, who, not finding the world into which he had been born thirty-five years before particularly to his liking, had rearranged it in his mind, and recast himself as a retiring scholarly gentleman of the nineteenth century. In our family he found a kind of verification for this myth, and spent hours by the fire in the little house, the dog at his feet, reading one of the dusty history books he loved, smoking cigarettes (Camels), sipping a bourbon, looking up occasionally to inject a wry, acerbic remark into the conversation. His self-created world cast us all as landed gentry, and our aging retriever, Max, as reigning monarch. We had had Max since he was a puppy, and scenes from his life had become a kind of family lore: the time he gave the beagle from up the street a thrashing and was subsequently taken to court; his trick, when we returned home from school, of leaping up and snatching the hats off the tops of our heads; the solitary roamings of his youth, in which he would cross the frozen river in wintertime and wander through the town for days, visiting a succession of females, until we would finally find him, trotting along the road in a distant part of town. The tragedy of his life came when another dog of ours, Daphne, with whom he was conspicuously in love, was hit by a car in front of our house and killed. The next morning, he went out to the spot where she had last been seen and barked clouds of breath into the thin morning air, and in her absence he fell into a depression from which only now, toward the end of his life, he had begun to recover. In our house, Max had a way of becoming the center of attention, the focus of our affection as if, unable to show our feelings directly to each other, we used him as the medium through which we revealed our love.

"He's *it*," Farnsworth said once, leaning forward and petting Max softly on the top of the head.

"He's what?" my mother asked.

"He's what!" said Farnsworth in mock indignation, his head tilting sideways like a bird's. "Why, well, he's king, of course. What else?"

For all his peculiarities, Farnsworth was outwardly steady, and addicted to the familiar in a reassuring way. Although he drank habitually and to excess, by temperament and personality he was rather sober, and his intelligence was not visibly dulled by drinking. Like an experimental car that has been adapted to run on synthetic fuel, Farnsworth seemed to have made a chemical adjustment to alcohol, which, at the expense of his body, served some deeper part of his unhappy soul. The signs of his illness were physical—his feet hurt, and his eyes did not always work as they should. He moved through the world slowly and deliberately, his motions polished by habit and a sullen reluctance to do anything too far removed from normal routine.

That spring, on Easter—the day on which, through a conjunction of good weather and added manpower, we had traditionally fixed the tennis court—Farnsworth put in an appearance, amused by this annual ritual of renewal: people raking, leaning over twisted tapes, pushing nails through them and into the soft, sun-warmed clay. At my sister's coaxing he pushed a few nails himself, arguing the entire time with her over the proper technique, and then, as if this simple activity had reactivated some private thought that needed mulling over, he subsided onto one of the nearby benches, his bare feet protruding from the legs of his pants. Several tennis-playing neighbors appeared, and a copy of the Encyclopaedia Britannica was brought up from the house, its fluttering pages held open with a hammer to "Pythagoras" while two grown men tried to recall the high-school mathematics required to make the court perfectly square.

"A squared plus B squared equals C squared," Farnsworth muttered from the bench.

"Well, we *know* that," said Mr. Walters, an affable computer expert from town. "That's not the problem, exactly."

Finally, after all the angles had been figured out, crucial corners nailed down, the moldy net dragged out of the barn and strung up, a ceremonial tennis ball stroked a few times across it, the impromptu crew, softened by beer and the surprisingly hot sun, dispersed and drifted down to the house for another drink. It was my mother who actually completed the job, working alone in the following days. She tapped in the remaining nails, pulled weeds and raked the clay, and pushed a heavy roller across the court, pressing it hard and smooth. "Well, the tennis court's in great shape," she cheerfully announced a week later, neglecting to mention that it was she who had made it so.

Although essentially alone, my mother was not at a loss for suitors. The rash of separation and divorce that had swept through my parents' friends had left a handful of husbands spouseless, and they, perhaps remembering some moment on a ski trip to the Adirondacks, recalling my mother's charm or beauty, would now and then appear in the little house for dinner or a drink. Arriving home, I would find my mother and one of these men at opposite ends of the couch, cigarette smoke rising from the ashtray in swirls shaped like question marks, and often something in the way they were sitting, or in the moment of adjustment that accompanied my unexpected entrance, suggested there was more than politics in the air. But then, as if our roles had been reversed and I were parental authority, the final crushing blow to possibility, the man would be sent away—a sudden lightness filling his steps, as if he were secretly relieved that what he had come in search of was not to be found.

It was during the summer that Mr. Walters began to make regular visits to our house. His sudden appearances were usually veiled in some good-natured errand—returning a hammer or borrowing a saw—but the frequency of his visits and the radiant look of expectation that accompanied his cheerful walk up the lawn, the sudden flush of color that came into his cheeks when he saw my mother suggested something else. They would sit in the kitchen of the little house, sipping coffee and talking, and as quickly as he appeared he would stride back across the lawn, wave good-bye, and speed off in his car, leaving a halo of dust hovering over the drive and a palpable silence, which my sister Susan would disrupt with an audible clearing of her throat.

"Never you mind," my mother would say from the kitchen, her voice strangely muted by the intervening panes of glass. "Never you mind."

But her meetings with Mr. Walters became more frequent and transparent; she would pass him as he walked to the train station and give him a ride—not to the station but all the way into town, where they would sit for half an hour in a coffee shop before he had to go to work. Mr. Walters was married, and so my mother was subjected to some mild forms of ostracism by some of her previous friends. She was no longer invited to certain parties, and as a family we were excluded from the Ludlows' annual Fourth of July party, an event I had gone to since I was a child. But as a family we were also held closer somehow, pressed toward a common center, as if, keepers of this same secret, we, too, were guilty—accomplices by association. The little house became our refuge, the place where we were safe, protected from the disapproving eyes of the town, and from where we disapproved of them.

In late summer, about a year or so after my father left, Lea left Farnsworth and moved into the barn. Although she still loved him, it had become apparent that she could not help him, and that his depression was bringing her down with him. The source of his unhappiness was deep

and hidden, like the hot core of a burning star, and knew
no consolation or solace, as if its own exhaustion were
the only thing that could put it out. Once employed as
a high-school science teacher, he had lost his job about
the time that they were married after a conflict with the
head of his department, and since then he had showed
little desire for another job, or faith in his ability to find
one. And after my sister left him, he lived in an increasingly private vacuum of alcohol and books, speaking only
to the shopkeepers who sold him his staples. Occasionally
he came over to the little house for dinner, but when
Lea was there he often would not want to leave, though
this was expressed less by words than by a silent reluctance to get out of the chair in which he was sitting.

"Your sister and I are finished," he said to me one night
as I drove him back along the road to his house. "But I
wish there was some way I could see more of you guys—
your family." I could feel him looking over at me through
the darkness.

I didn't know what to say. "I know. "It's hard for Lea,
that's all."

"I know."

The car swept through the deserted streets of the town.
I pulled up at the curb in front of the grocery store, over
which Farnsworth lived.

"Well, I'll come over for tea sometime."

"You do that," Farnsworth answered, reaching out to
shake my extended hand. "And thank you, Peter. I'm
grateful." He laughed his soft, self-deprecating laugh and
climbed wearily out of the car.

"Take care of yourself," I called after him.

"I'll try," said Farnsworth, and, as if in acknowledg-

ment of my concern, he laughed again, and headed for
the door.

Early the next fall, I was sitting in the kitchen of the little
house, sipping a cup of tepid coffee, looking out through
the panes of glass to the yard. It was Sunday, raining,
and a warm wind was blowing through the tops of the
trees. For reasons I did not understand, my mother was
frantically cleaning the house—making beds, sweeping
floors, puffing up pillows—pausing only to take a drag
from her cigarette or a sip from a glass filled with a sus-
picious-looking transparent liquid. She was in the attic,
cleaning out a closet, when I saw the shadowy figure of
a man in a hat and carrying a small suitcase coming up
the driveway and across the lawn. He came in the door
without knocking, stomped his feet on the mat, and
looked up, his cheeks flushed.

"Why, hello," he said, apparently surprised to see me.
It was Mr. Walters. "Is your mother here?"

Just then my mother came walking quickly into the
kitchen, and, seeing him, made a dramatic gesture of
relief. "Excuse us," she said, kissing him and then turning
back to me with an amused expression of apology. "I'm
so relieved. How did you get here?" she asked him.

"Well, it was quite simple, really," Mr. Walters said. "I
walked."

That night he stayed for dinner and never went home.
He had told his children that morning, his wife the night
before, and then he just left, walking the two miles to
our house—down Landon Street, along the edge of the
river, over the bridge, and onto Blind Man's Lane, which
wound the final mile to our house. "It was really quite

lovely," Mr. Walters said. "Squawking ducks, rain, falling leaves, wind." The matter-of-fact simplicity with which he recounted these events created in my mother a giddy disbelief—a kind of nervous ebullience. The windows of the little house shook and rattled in the wind, rain beating off the panes, candles flickering in the faint breezes that found their way in.

"You just *left?*" Lea asked.

"Well, yes. Basically. I mean they knew I was going. What's wrong with that?" Mr. Walters said, and he laughed, as if for the first time realizing the implications of his two-mile walk.

Lea admonished my mother for being so transparently happy.

"I'm sorry, I can't help it," she said, and went into the kitchen and began to wash the dishes. Mr. Walters came in and hugged her—a sight so odd I had to look away.

"We're going to get an apartment in Litchfield," my mother told me that evening as she drove me to the train. "And wait for the smoke to clear. It will make it easier on everyone."

"How did his wife take it?"

"Well, not too well, really, but Jim expected that. She was very angry, understandably."

"What about the kids?"

"I don't know, really. We haven't had time to talk about it. I'm still in a state of shock."

"And Mr. Walters is going to spend the night?"

"He has to—where else?" Her little car swung through the darkness and rain, past the landmarks of my child-hood—Sherman's Drugstore, the library, the movie theater, the church—past the street on which, earlier that day, Mr. Walters had lived. She stopped in front of the train station.

"Well, good luck," I said lamely, leaning back into the car to kiss her.

"Well, *you* don't worry about it," she said. "It's not your problem."

"I won't," I said, and, relieved to be leaving, sprinted off to the train.

That year, for lack of a large enough room in the little house or in my mother's apartment, we had Thanksgiving in the barn. My mother cleaned it and arranged some extra furniture in the semblance of a living room, and she placed our old dining-room table at the farthest end, beside the wood stove. We lit the stove that morning, filling the room with smoke in an effort to bring the temperature up to a reasonable level of warmth. My aunt, my mother's sister—a woman who had outlived her happy husband and their unhappy marriage—had refused to come: a one-woman show of disapproval against Mr. Walters's leaving his wife, against my mother's hand in their now abandoned marriage. But Mr. Walters's sister and her husband drove over from Boonton, in the northern part of the state. Lea had gone to Pennsylvania to visit my grandmother, but Farnsworth came, and Susan and her boyfriend drove out from the city. In the wood-heated barn the miscellaneous parts of our scattered family gathered in a cheerful semblance of a cohesive whole. Max fell asleep on the floor, and the components of dinner—pots of mashed potatoes, cranberries, squash, bottles of wine, and, last of all, the heroic, steaming turkey—were comically carried from the kitchen of the little house across the tundra-like surface of the yard. Farnsworth said grace. Dinner was uneventful, and when it was over, before coffee and dessert, we spilled out of the barn for a walk.

It was a leaden, overcast day, and Max and a couple of our neighbor's dogs ran out along the road before us, their tails waving like flags, the only flecks of color in the muted, sombre landscape. The marsh stretched away on either side, and the dogs ran off across it, leaping over creeks, sniffing the mud, making the bushes sway, and then reemerging, running back to us, as if for approval of their happiness. When we reached the gate of the Coopers' estate, marked "Private Property," my mother, in a faintly anarchic spirit and buoyed by our numbers, insisted that we pass through. The iron gate swung open with a squeal, and we continued, the party extending along the narrow strip of asphalt road, breaking off in pockets of conversation and laughter as someone leapt to catch a bouncing ball, chased a dog, or broke into an amused, incongruous run. Farnsworth had picked up an old, gnarled stick and was trying to explain to Susan why every gentleman should have a cane.

"Well, so he can fend off robbers, or dogs," he said. "Or so he won't fall down. Oh, Christ, I don't know why every gentleman should have a cane. He just does, and if he doesn't, he's not a gentleman!" He laughed, and tossed the stick off to the side of the road.

We were the only moving things around, and our presence seemed to take on exaggerated importance, as if we were the last people on earth. We veered off the road down a path to an enormous open field stretching away to the marsh. In the distance was the white edge of sand dunes, the thin blue edge of the sea. We stopped and stared, and then, in silent agreement, drifted back in the direction we had come.

Back in the barn, after coffee and dessert, Susan, her boyfriend, Farnsworth, and I collapsed onto the over-stuffed couches and made adolescent jokes about turkey—"first the turkey and then the surprise"—and gave in to that feeling of exhaustion that comes from over-eating. But there was something in the way that Farnsworth sat and looked that suggested he really was exhausted, that this was a game to everyone but him. He had told me that recently he'd been having trouble sleeping, and would sit up half the night instead, drinking and reading. And on days when he came to our house he often seemed to be in some sort of trance, as if what was happening to him were just the extension of a baffling dream.

Several months later, while skiing with an old college friend in Utah, I learned that Farnsworth had died. The news came to me on the phone, during lunch, amid the din and clatter of crashing plates, the laughter of sunburned skiers, the sizzle of food in an alpine lodge halfway up the mountain. It was Susan who called, and her voice was clear and cheerful, as if to soften what she had to report. Oddly, I felt grateful to Farnsworth for giving me a chance to leave.

I packed my bag, and walked back down the mountain through the blur of my tears, carrying on a steady monologue to Farnsworth for being such an imbecile. On the bus to the airport, I struck up an effortless conversation with a woman whom, under different circumstances, I would have pursued. On a changeover in Atlanta, at 3 a.m., I had a couple of drinks in Farnsworth's honor, hoisting a glass of bourbon toward a waitress in a dimly lit airport bar. Later, from the plane window, my head pressed against the glass, I watched the glitter of land silently passing beneath me, a magically flat plain of twinkling lights, and the luminous starbursts of civilization.

Susan met me in New York, at the airport, and we drove the five hours north, up through the frozen landscape on a bitterly cold winter day, over familiar highways, along familiar roads to home: past the movie theater, church, train station, library, school, over the bridge, left, right, and then wobbling over the familiar bumps and turns of our road—up, over and down, and turning onto the crackling stone driveway. A crowd of people, pressed behind the greenhouse windows of the little house, silently waved. I crossed the frozen lawn and went in, collapsing in Lea's arms in an unexpected volley of tears, instantly making me the center of female solace. Recovered, I found in the living room everyone who had ever known Farnsworth, people who looked and talked like him. But they were standing around uncertainly, gathered in his absence instead of his presence, like witnesses to a magic trick that had finally worked, with the magician disappearing from their midst forever.

That spring, I took a term off from college and moved to New York and worked as a copyboy on a newspaper. On April 1st, Lea's birthday, I called home during a break at work to wish her a happy birthday. She thanked me for calling but said that Max had played an April Fool joke on everyone: he had disappeared a couple of nights before, and had turned up that morning on the marsh, looking like a clump of peat, bloated and damp from several salty washings of the tides. The precise cause of his death, like Farnsworth's, was uncertain. Had he eaten too much of the neighbor's horse grain, and had a heart attack, or was he simply exhausted from living a life happily devoted to impulse?

I received this news badly, too, and cried into the pay phone at which I was standing. I took it as a rather unnecessary signal that my childhood, after twenty years, was finally over. We had got Max as a puppy the autumn we moved to the big house, so I had never lived at home without him. The next time I went home I was prepared for Max's absence but not for the silence, the sound of wind blowing through the tops of the trees, and the fact that I had no one to take walks with.

Lea had met Farnsworth when she was seventeen, and married when she was twenty-one, and now, having expended all her love, hope, and sorrow while he was living, in widowhood she found her grief transformed into a kind of spiritual release, and returned to an adolescence she had previously missed. She continued to live in the barn, bought herself a moped, painted, drew, listened to reggae, and, happy to be alone, became a kind of overseer of nature, collecting the bleached bones of deer, the cough balls of owls she found in fields and woods around the house. Her corner of the barn became a small museum for unusual artifacts, among them several small wooden sculptures of monastic figures that Farnsworth had painstakingly carved and painted as a child.

By that summer, the self-imposed exile of my mother and Mr. Walters had become pointless, and they moved back into the little house. In the fall, my mother gleefully evicted the tenants from the big white house and, with Mr. Walters, moved back in. She hired a mover this time, and oversaw two lumbering high-school students as they reversed our labors of two years before. After the cottage, its large empty spaces were unexpected, like finding something you had never realized you had lost. Their friends from town gradually adapted to the change, and slowly crept back into their world. The tennis court was revived on Easter, and that spring enjoyed a small renaissance, hosting weekend doubles matches between the odds and ends of scattered couples.

The wedding was small, and took place on a warm, balmy day in early June. The tide in the creek was high. The grass was not fully green, and a trace of spring's thinness still lingered on the trees. The doors of the house were left open, and its rooms were filled with a soft, summer light and the curtains billowed in the wind. My two sisters were there, my aunt, several cousins, and, their presence tinged with reticence, Mr. Walters's two adolescent children. In bare feet, we strolled across the lawn sipping champagne and firing bottle rockets into the creek. Chairs were set up on the porch, and at the appointed hour we gathered there as Mr. Walters and my mother stood with the minister between bouquets of flowers to exchange their vows. The sound of wind could be heard in the trees, then a car passing on the road, the flap of a distant sail. When my mother spoke it was with a voice that I had never heard, the words at once soft and clear, like a bell, and filled with the shy, hopeful promise of a child. Her words seemed to hover over the grass and drift away, settling in the garden like snow. It was a voice, I realized, that was much younger than hers, that she had used only once before, twenty-odd years ago, but that now, on this spring morning of early June, had not faded with the intervening years.

Due Cappuccini

O n their first night in Capua Anna's uncle asked Michael, with Anna serving as interpreter, if he believed in "the sanctity of marriage." Uncle Enzo was rather small and stern-looking, and after he asked the question his eyes seemed to glitter in amused expectation of Michael's response. He fumbled his way through a vague and swirling answer, which he then heard translated into Anna's lilting, beautiful Italian. The uncle nodded in response but did not seem entirely satisfied, and he was about to ask another question when his two children appeared—a pair of angelic boys in what looked like their Sunday best—and mercifully ended the inquisition. Michael and Anna finished their coffee and dessert, thanked Anna's aunt, and slipped into their own part of the house—an unused wing that, Anna had explained bitterly, her uncle intended to renovate and rent out for income. It was not until later that the strangeness of the question began to irritate Michael.

"What does he mean, anyway, 'the sanctity of marriage'?"

"Don't listen to him," said Anna. "I told you he's an idiot."

"I know that, but what does he mean? That God comes down and touches you and tells you to get married? Or that you never get divorced even though you hate each other's guts, or that you never look at your secretary's bottom? And are you supposed to dress your kids up like birthday cakes and parade them through the square after dinner so everyone can see how perfect you are?"

"Come on," Anna said, and laughed. "Like birthday cakes? They didn't look like that."

"They did! Did you see them? You'd think the pope was coming."

"That's just them," Anna said defensively. "That's just here. I keep telling you. It's not New York. There's nothing wrong with it."

"I know. It's fine. But he doesn't have to start cross-examining me the minute I show up with his niece. I hadn't even finished my pasta and he starts interrogating me about my morals."

"That's just him. I told you. He's a jerk. Penzo—that's what we used to call him when we were little. We had a rabbit named that. That's what he is, really. A little, stupid rabbit."

"I agree," said Michael.

But the next night after dinner, it was Anna's aunt who did the talking. While Michael sat sipping his coffee, trying not to reach for another pastry, and Uncle Penzo sat staring at his wife with that same look of expectation, Anna and her aunt started in on a long, deliberate conversation, to which Michael listened calmly, as if he understood. He had no idea what they were saying, but he could tell it was something important, and he could tell by her tone of voice that Anna was growing increasingly agitated. Their voices slowly swelled in the tiny, overheated room, and Penzo continued to sit, still and wordless, until the whole fragile structure of civility suddenly collapsed. Like two thunderclouds filled with rain, Anna and her aunt stood up and began to unleash torrents of anger onto each other, their arms gesturing, carving shapes in midair, their voices filling the room with desperate strains of outrage and incomprehension. Anna stalked away, turned, ran at her aunt, and stopped just short of collision. The children cowered behind a half-open door, and Uncle Penzo remained silent—even when Anna turned her attention to him, a string of words flowing from her mouth in a wonderful ornate scroll of loathing and contempt. When her speech was finished, she rushed the aunt once more, turned, and strode powerfully out of the room. Michael sat for a moment longer and then, realizing his allegiances were elsewhere, downed the last of his coffee, said, "*Scusi,*" and followed her.

"Come on," she said, pulling on her coat. "Let's get out of here."

Together, they walked in silence down the ancient stone staircase of the house, out through the heavy wooden door, and into the hushed streets of the town. They turned left, then right, and followed a narrow alley to the cool, gray spaces by the river, where a few old men fished in the murky twilight. Insects skittered along the top of the water, and a few teenagers on motorbikes loitered by a signpost and made faint hissing sounds to Anna as they passed.

"*Cretino. Imbecille,*" Anna said, loud enough for them to hear, slapping one hand against an upraised arm in a classic Italian salute of disrespect. The boys pointed and laughed.

"Sh-h-h," Michael said. "They'll take it out on me. And what was that all about, anyway? What were you and your aunt fighting about?"

"Did you see the way he just sat there, without opening his little, disgusting mouth? He made her say it because he's too much of a coward himself. That's the way he always is. My grandmother hated him for it. If she could see what he's done to her house she'd turn over in her grave. I hate him," she concluded bitterly.

"I know that, but what were you fighting about? I don't speak the language, remember?"

"They don't want us to stay there. They said we can't stay together because we're not married. They want me to sleep with the children."

"What did you say?"

"I told her it was just as much my parents' house as it was hers. My granny left it to both families, and we're going to stay there as long as we want. It's none of their business where we sleep, and we're going to stay until we want to leave. Penzo just sat there like a little worm. Did you see him? He always makes her do the talking."

"Maybe it was her idea."

"Are you kidding? She's not like that. He made her do it. I know him. 'For the sake of the children,' she told me! That's sick. They're the ones who are corrupting the children with their sick ideas."

Down by the river, the fishermen were packing up their things, and bats, or birds—blurs in the half-light—were swooping over the murky water.

"Wow. I've never seen anything like that before," Michael said, shaking his head.

"Like what?"

"Like two grown women trying to tear each other's heads off." He reached out and touched her broad, strong back, still damp from her exertions.

"Welcome to Italy," Anna said softly, and then slowly, surely, started to cry.

In fact, they had been in Italy for weeks. They had arrived almost a month before, on a hot summer morning, at a quiet underused airport outside Rome. And there, groggy with sleeplessness and the odd unreality of being in a strange place, Michael was moved by a powerful medley of first impressions: the hazy, undulating line of distant, bluish mountains; the dusty red of flowers that lined the airport drive; the happy, agitated twitter of Italian birds; the burned, sweet smell of the ancient, umber earth. Everything seemed old.

With their few bags, they made their way through customs, walked down the drive, and held out their arms at the first passing car. It stopped, and they found themselves rolling through the lovely Italian landscape, filled with pine trees shaped like hats, distant aqueducts, and crumbling reddish ruins that seemed to crowd the narrow road. They swept past the Colosseum and veered into the center of town, where the driver dropped them off at the railroad station.

They took a train to Rimini, and later that afternoon they boarded another train which carried them up over rugged, stony mountains, through sun-baked cities and crumbling towns, and left them at a small seaside resort on the Adriatic. There they spent a happy week with Anna's other relatives—on her father's side—flopping in the warm, salty Mediterranean waves, playing Ping-Pong, eating enormous peaches that grew on a slender, overladen tree in the backyard. It was a sandy little town filled with the scent of pine trees, and with rotund vacationing Germans and pretty brown-skinned girls in bikinis who glided around like circus performers, standing up on the backs of other people's bicycles. In the middle of town there was a sandy square with a kiosk that reminded Michael of an illustration in his old high-school French book: a mustachioed man with a cane forever buying a copy of the morning paper.

Then they took off on a haphazard tour of the country: up to Verona, over to Padua, and then—hitchiking—on to Venice. They didn't have much money, or felt as if they didn't, and so usually slept out-of-doors—in small, secluded parks, or under pine trees, or on grassy verges not far from the road. In Venice, they slept in a stone square near the train station, along with other travelers, and in the morning they were wakened by policemen prodding everyone awake with nightsticks before the tourists arrived. Anna looked up from her sleeping bag and said, "*Due cappuccini e brioches, per favore?*," but the policeman didn't even smile.

It turned out that neither of them was the camping

type, and they were both more needy of sheets and beds than they had imagined. And after a week of sleepless, flea-bitten nights and of days spent stumbling around with their backpacks they were exhausted. At a little dusty train station in the middle of nowhere, they got into a fight, and decided to take the train south and spend the rest of their time in the town where Anna had spent much of her childhood. There, at least, they would have a place to sleep—a base from which they could make excursions to the surrounding towns and countryside. On their way, they stopped in Florence, Rome, and Naples, before taking a little bouncy bus the final hour to their destination. Anna's family on her mother's side had lived here for generations. Anna had been closest to her grandmother, but she had died several years before, and Anna's grandfather had never really recovered from the time he had spent in a prison camp during the First World War. He lived in a small room on the second floor, and on their first day Michael had seen him from the street—a small, grinning man with no teeth, waving down from the window as though he were still held captive. Anna later tried to visit him, but he didn't even remember her name.

After the scene with her aunt, Anna locked the connecting door to their part of the house and vowed not to leave until it was time to go back to New York. The thought of resuming their wanderings was not appealing to Michael, either, and the presence of a bed, a roof, a place to spend their nights and days outweighed the pressures of social and familial disapproval. The following morning, Anna's aunt slipped a short, cool note under the door, saying that Anna had left some laundry in the kitchen and could pick it up later that afternoon, when the family was out. In the days that followed, now and then they would hear the voices of Penzo and his wife through the wall, or catch glimpses of the family through the window as they were going out for a walk, and one evening they ran into one of the boys, Beppe, at the stationery store, buying some pencils for school. Anna crouched down and tried to talk with him, but he seemed to be acting under orders not to associate with her, and he looked relieved when she finally kissed him on the cheek and sent him on his way.

"That bitch," Anna said. "She won't even let me talk to my own cousin."

From the store, they turned in the other direction and walked down into the main square of town. Everyone was out on the streets—young married couples, children on their bicycles, clumps of old men in black, talking and gesturing and leaning back in their chairs against the crumbling walls of the church. The younger men, sitting on their motorcycles or leaning against signposts, whistled or hissed or murmured soft, suggestive remarks to Anna as she passed. Even the older men sometimes stopped in their tracks and stared at her, as if it were their obligation, or male duty, to do so. Now and then, Michael would stop and stare defiantly back at them.

"Stop!" Anna said firmly. "That's what they want."

"Can't they see you're with someone?" Michael asked, annoyed. "What if you were married? They stare at people's wives?"

"They can tell we're not married. And they can tell you're not from here. That's why they whistle."

"How can they tell I'm not from here?" Michael asked, looking down at his clothes. "I look Italian."

Anna laughed—a single loud monosyllable of mirth. "Ha! You look like you just walked out of a comic book, with your freckles and old tennis shoes. You look like Jughead or Popeye."

"Thanks a lot. Do I make fun of you in New York?"

"No, why would you? Beauty is universal," she said, and laughed at the pleasant truth of her remark. Michael tried to think of a retort but couldn't: it was true. In New York, she looked as if she belonged, too.

From the square they walked down to the river, where there were fewer people and where the last pale light of day lingered on the broad, smooth expanse of water. They sat on a bench until nightfall, when the air turned cool and still, and tiny, invisible bugs began to bite at Anna's legs and arms. Then, to their surprise, the moon appeared—an enormous, swollen ball rising up through the trees. Michael had never seen the moon so large or such a color—an eerie reddish yellow, like an exotic ripening fruit.

"Wow," Michael said softly. "Why is it so large?"

"It's pregnant—that's what my grandmother used to tell us," Anna said, and with that they stood and made their way back toward the house.

In their travels around town, they would now and then run into people Anna knew. The woman in the bakery went into a long reminiscence about how she knew Anna when Anna was only as tall as a loaf of bread and used to come in with her grandmother. And in the stationery store a plump, homely girl took a few minutes studying

Anna's smiling face before collapsing onto her shoulder
with a long, happy wail—"Annnnnaaaa!" Already, word
of Anna's fight with her aunt had sifted down to the ears
of the girl in the stationery store, who listened closely as
Anna recounted her own version of the story, and nodded
sympathetically when it was over. But Anna was not
convinced.

"She's just like the rest of them," she said to Michael
when they left. "I could tell by the way she kept nodding,
like a puppet. They all start screwing when they're fourteen, out in the hayfields, but if your boyfriend spends
the night, forget it—you're the village whore. It's O.K.
for the men, but if a girl gets pregnant nobody will marry
her. In Sicily they cut a chicken's head off over the bed
the day after the wedding just in case, so everyone thinks
the bride's a virgin. If she isn't, the man might divorce
her, even though he's been with half her sisters."

In the house next to Anna's, there was an old woman
with a pleasant wrinkled face, and when Anna and Michael came in from the town she would often be sitting
out on the street, in front of her door, and they would
stop and talk with her. "*Americano, si?*" she said once,
smiling up at Michael, rolling the word around in her
mouth like a grape, to see how it tasted. She had been
best friends with Anna's grandmother but was a widow
now, and always dressed in black. "*Americano!*" she repeated, and she was still nodding when they stepped
through the old wooden door into the house.

One morning Michael woke to a strange rumble, like
an earthquake gathering force, through which he discerned the steady clump of a horse's hooves. "What's
that?" he said, sitting up in bed. Anna stirred beside him,

then climbed over him and went to the window, naked. It saddened him to notice that the tan she had carefully worked on at the seaside was already beginning to fade to a dull, New York gray.

"Oh, it's the fruit seller!" she said happily. "Look, quick." Michael moved to the window, and there below, on the cobbled streets, was an ancient, grizzled horse in harness, pulling a long, flat cart laden with vegetables and fruit; an old man in a battered hat was holding the reins.

"Oh, I wish I had a basket," Anna said in a voice that sounded like a little girl's. "You lower it on a rope with your money, and he puts in the fruit and you raise it back up. That's how my granny used to buy her things. I didn't know he was around anymore."

Anna yelled something down and made a gesture of apology. The old man smiled, waved, snapped the reins. The horse stepped forward and, with another rumble, all the fruits and vegetables went rolling down the street.

"Next time," Anna said wistfully.

Cut off from the family, they were obliged to find their own breakfast, and usually they would go to one of the small cafés off the main square of town. There they would order two cappuccinos and a couple of pastries and sit in the cool blue shade, looking out through the window as the town slowly came to life. An old bald man brought them their coffee and then went about his business with the enormous steaming machines. At a nearby table a couple of elderly men would begin their morning game of dominoes, and a younger man in a blue uniform would come in, down a cup of espresso as though it were medicine, and go out. It was a relief for Michael and Anna to be out of the house, where they were not welcome, and off the streets, where the boys whistled and old women murmured and their husbands stood around in little clumps staring at Anna. In the café, at least, they were alone.

A few blocks away, halfway between the river and the main part of town, there was another square—old and beautiful, surrounded by a stone colonnade and red tiled roofs—which in the mornings would fill up with carts and horses as the farmers from the countryside brought in their fruits and vegetables for market. On their way back from breakfast, Anna and Michael would stop there and buy food for the day—bread and mozzarella cheese made from buffalo milk, bags of grapes and olives and peaches. From the square, they cut back through a narrow alley to the house and went in through the Romanesque arch that spanned the front door. The arch, and the house itself, Anna reported casually, dated from the second half of the fifteen hundreds—a fact that amazed and moved Michael more than all the monuments he had seen in Rome. Once inside, they would spend the morning in their pleasant, old-fashioned room, still decorated as it had been when Anna was a child: antique furniture, lace curtains, old faded photographs of Anna's grandparents when they were young. There were several windows looking out through the thick stone walls onto the alley below, and through them they could hear people from the surrounding buildings, the clink of pots and pans, a barking dog, footsteps, a passing bicycle.

"There used to be a lemon tree here," Anna said once. "The lemons would come right in the window, and when I was little I used to sit there knitting or sewing or peeling

142

potatoes for Granny. Everything was filled with lemon smell. But then my granny died, and that stupid little jerk married my auntie and cut down the tree—'to let in the light,' he said. I could kill him."

"How come she married him if he's such an idiot?"

"Because there was no one else. She was getting desperate. She was thirty five, and in this town that's like being a hundred. Everyone kept asking her when she was getting married, and so when that little worm came around she had no choice. Then she got pregnant, so they got married."

"*She* got pregnant before she was married, and she's telling you not to sleep with your boyfriend?"

"Of course," Anna said. "It's like that. Why do you think I got so mad? That's why we were fighting. She told me my granny would roll over in her grave if she knew my boyfriend slept here. I didn't want to say it, but then I got so mad I couldn't help it: I told her to leave my granny out of it, and then I asked her how come Beppe was born only four months after they were married, if she was such a good Catholic. Why do you think Penzo just sat there as if he had eaten a frog? I'm surprised he could even make her pregnant."

They would spend the rest of the morning in this dark, quiet room—Michael reading, or writing letters home, Anna washing clothes or drawing or taking a bath and then lying, clean and white and naked, in the pale light that fell through the window. Strangely, it was in this novel state of exile that Michael got the first, distant taste—like an unfamiliar fragrance—of what it must feel like to be married. For the first time since he had met her, almost two years before, they spent all of their time together.

At noon, after the horn from the bicycle factory—the main industrial edifice of the town—sounded, discharging its workers for siesta, they would get dressed and go out again into the now deserted streets. The little stone square, filled with hundreds of people only an hour before, was now empty—the shop windows boarded up, the carts and men and animals gone—and on the cobblestones were the only clues that there had been a market that day: a brown leaf of lettuce, a squashed grape, a dirty olive, a fish skin drying in the sun. A flock of pigeons was always there, picking crumbs from the ground where the bread cart had been, or sitting on the fountain, basking in the heat of the early-autumn sun. When Michael and Anna appeared at the far end of the square, the pigeons leapt up, and, with the sound of laundry flapping in the wind, wheeled once, twice, above them and then settled into the chinks and gaps and shadows of the red tiled roofs. In these hot midday hours, released from its usual inhabitants, the town became their own.

They would pass through the sun-baked square, pause by the fountain, then continue across to the river. From inside the shuttered houses they would hear the sounds of domestic life—the tinkling of forks and knives, muffled voices, a crying child, the sonorous drone of a TV. They would drift along with a pleasant sensation of truancy, of being in a place where they did not belong. Now and then, they would come upon an old woman sitting in the shade of her front door, and as they passed they could feel the heat of her questioning, disapproving gaze on their backs.

They would follow the river until it became too hot, and turn back into the relative cool of the streets and walk until they reached their end—a shady vacant lot that gave way to the dusty green fields that surrounded the town. They would pause and look out, then turn and walk back through the meandering streets toward home. By the time they reached the main square the town would be stirring back to life—workers in blue uniforms drifting toward the factory, schoolchildren waiting for the stationery store to reopen so they could buy their penny candy, the old men unlocking their cafés, letting Michael and Anna in for another cappuccino.

One afternoon on their way home they stopped to visit a friendly, progressive priest Anna had known since childhood. He was a handsome young man in glasses, who moonlighted as a poet—"spiritual poems," he clarified. In his book-filled office at the back of the church, he greeted them warmly, and then listened as Anna recounted the story of her fight with her aunt and the ensuing estrangement from the family. He advised her not to worry and explained to Michael in broken English that the town was rather an old-fashioned one, and that he shouldn't take it personally. "It will pass," he reassured them. "It will pass." He thanked them for coming, encouraged them to visit again, and gave Anna a long, affectionate hug, which—to Michael, at least—did not seem entirely priestly.

"Just because you put on a black robe desn't mean you don't have feelings," Anna said afterward.

"Yeah, but it doesn't mean you have to hug your female parishioners when they come for moral guidance, either. Maybe he *should* have been a poet."

"Maybe you should have been a priest," Anna suggested, "if you have such high morals." Then she smiled.

Michael groped for a retort but couldn't find one.

But after their visit with the priest it seemed to him that people no longer stared at them with the same curiosity as before. Perhaps they had grown accustomed to the sight of them, or perhaps it was because Michael had assumed a more aggressive stance, and now tightly held Anna's arm as they walked, the way he had seen the men in town walk with their wives. He had also begun to dress more conservatively, forsaking jeans and shorts for his one pair of good pants, and Anna had begun to wear skirts and sandals instead of pants and sneakers. As a joke, Anna sometimes switched a big gaudy ring she had bought at a SoHo flea market to the ring finger of her left hand, and whenever anyone stared at them she would make the ring more visible, and smile the contented sardonic smile of matrimony. In the evenings, they began to walk more slowly, and no longer sought the privacy of the river but paraded straight through the main square of town. One night they saw Anna's aunt and uncle and the two children—all dressed in white, like a flock of angels—eating ice-cream cones. Neither they nor Anna nor Michael gave a sign of recognition, but on the way back across the square, as families and stray couples began to trickle home and the murmur of night began to replace the bustle of evening, Michael saw the family again, and this time he looked over at the aunt, who, seeing him, smiled the strange, enigmatic smile of a Madonna he had seen in the local museum.

When they arrived back at the old stone doorway, the woman from next door was sitting out in her chair, and they were obliged to stop and talk with her. Michael stood on the street and distractedly listened, looking off to where some small children were playing with a mangy dog, and through the texture of their conversation—like the distant, incomprehensible sound of a babbling stream—he could make out only two words that he knew: *"Due cappuccini, due cappuccini!"* the old woman kept saying excitedly, waving two fingers in the air as if in illustration. Her old eyes opened wide, and she looked up at Michael with a wry, crooked smile.

Anna laughed halfheartedly and rolled her eyes at Michael and then toward the door. *"Due cappuccini!"* the woman repeated. Anna said good night and led Michael up the stairs and into the house.

"Jesus Christ," she said when they were inside. "Did you hear all that? *'Due cappuccini, due cappuccini!'* Old bag. Why doesn't she leave us alone?"

"Why? What did she say?"

"She said that the old man from the café, the bald one, is her son-in-law. Every morning we come in, he told her. *'Due cappuccini, due cappuccini!* Every morning it's the same."

"So? What's wrong with that?"

"What's wrong with *us* that we have to go out? What's wrong with our family? Can't they make cappuccino at home? Good girls don't go out for breakfast. Good girls don't have breakfast with their boyfriends. That's what she was telling me: she has her eye on us. She knows what happened, but she doesn't want to say it, so she comes up with that stupid story about cappuccino. And all the old men in town have been talking about us."

"Why don't they mind their own business?"

"It *is* their business," Anna said simply. "They live here."

The idea came to Michael in the undulating folds of darkness, in the fuzzy place between a sleepy thought and a thoughtless dream—a memory of home, or a premonition of things to come. It was all a pleasant blur—an unusually vivid dream, in which his own mother and father, long divorced and living in different states, were helping him shingle, with bundles of hay, the side of a barn he somehow owned. And then there was a blissful childhood memory, distilled into the euphoric contours of a dream—the delicious, conflicting impulses of escape and capture as he swept across the lush green grass of the school yard, just beyond the plump, pretty hands of desperate Louise Martin. His knees went weak and buckled beneath him, and he rolled onto the cool grass, laughing, and let himself be captured. And then he was in the café with Anna as the first light of morning fell in through the window. The old man at the coffee machine pretended not to notice, and when they left would not let them pay. "Good customers, good customers," he said, in English, and waved them out the door. Then they were in the priest's study—Anna in her best dress, Michael in a suit and tie he had somehow borrowed from Uncle Penzo. The priest smiled broadly, hugged Anna, shook Michael's hand, and led them down through a smooth stone corridor to a small, sunlit garden, where a straw-hatted old man worked among the flowers. The man was asked to be a witness, and he smiled and dropped his trowel. Then they all disappeared into the cool, vaulted reaches of the church.

Michael woke to a distant half-familiar rumble, but before he had even opened his eyes he could feel Anna leaping up beside him, crawling over him, making her way to the corner of the room and the basket, to which, several days before, she had tied a long piece of string. Naked still, she ran to the window, exposing only her head, so that her breasts, visible only to Michael, hung from her torso like strange and wonderful fruit. She yelled something down to the street, and the rumbling stopped. She put some money in the basket and carefully lowered it down, like a fisherman letting out line.

"Ah, *due pesche, quattro mele, e un grappolo d'uva,*" she shouted, and a moment later she raised her basket with her catch—apples and grapes and peaches and a few pieces of change. "*Grazie, grazie,*" she yelled down, and waved. As the cart rumbled away, she took a bite of one of the peaches and, as if tasting part of her own past, closed her eyes and smiled.

Michael sat sleepily up on the edge of the bed. "Shall we go out for breakfast now?"

"What? Why?" Anna asked, almost hurt. "Aren't we staying here? That's why I bought the fruit."

"What about coffee?"

"We can have it here. Yesterday I found an old machine of Granny's and a hot plate in the closet. I bought some coffee and milk at the store. It was going to be a surprise," she said, pulling her nightgown on over her head.

Michael subsided onto the edge of the bed and, initially

regretting they were not to sit in the café that morning, silently acquiesced. In her new role as cappuccino-maker, Anna went about her business with renewed energy, murmuring to herself as she worked, like a child playing with dolls. *"Due cappuccini. . . . Un momento, per favore."* He had seldom seen her so happy.

"I had an interesting dream last night," Michael said softly, but she didn't seem to hear him.

"It's stuck, it's stuck," Anna said desperately, struggling with the machine. "I can't get the top off."

Michael took up the grimy old device, banged it once on the floor, and twisted it open.

"Grazie," Anna said, her happiness restored. "What dream?"

What dream? The question sounded as if it had come from someplace far away, and now seemed of little consequence. Anna, absorbed in her task, did not ask again, and Michael did not answer but sat in a pleasant, sleepy stupor, consumed by the domestic sounds that now enveloped him: the clinking of the coffeepot, the running water, the rustle of her nightgown as she passed, the slap of her bare feet on the cool stone tiles. And then the old machine began to hiss and sputter and make impatient sounds of escaping steam, filling the room with a rich, powerful smell that evoked for Michael some vague and irretrievable memory from his childhood. And then a plate of fruit, transformed into patterns of color, appeared on the table beside him, and with the endearing gesture of a waitress Anna leaned forward and poured him a cup of coffee. As she did so, the flimsy cloth of her nightgown fell away, briefly revealing to him the mysterious and beautiful contours of her bare, pale breasts. His fondness for her merged with gratitude and desire, and for once his feelings for Anna seemed justified, if only because they were having breakfast at home.

Social Studies

As the term wound down, Henry wound down too, or tried; but in his last week of classes he had finally run out of steam, or interest, or empathy, and the reams of student papers that had suddenly appeared on his desk swam before him in an unexpected blizzard of half-baked, poorly expressed ideas. He read them all, however, moved occasionally by a faint blush of sincerity and effort, and at the end added his own blurry remarks and a grade—usually one higher than he actually thought was deserved. But as he read his mind drifted, and he wondered if he was suffering from what they called, in the business, "teacher burnout," that condition of indifference and malaise that sets in after a few thousand students and—worse still—a handful of pasty administrators and their countless memos and meetings and veiled admonitions about Henry's grading policy ("inflated"), his refusal to use the traditional red pen in "marking" papers, or his reluctance to wear a tie. His life seemed to him a quagmire of rules, an endless and entangling web of things both he and his students ought and ought not do. His immediate superior was a jolly, roundish man expert in appeasing angry parents or making jokes at assemblies but deficient, Henry thought, at actually running a school. He gave off the scent of misused power, and Henry was always uncomfortable in his presence, and secretly relieved when he wandered back to his own end of the hall.

Now, though, it was Friday afternoon, and the term was finally over. The last of his students had long since filed out of his room, laughing and shrieking and wishing Mr. Veen, "Hen" as they liked to call him, a Merry Christmas; but that sublime moment of euphoria he had always felt as a student never came—only a slow, swollen fatigue and the certainty that, fourteen days hence, a whole new collage of smiling, adolescent faces would be filing back in.

He stuffed the last scattered papers into his briefcase, pulled on his coat and hat, and walked out to where Pete, an elderly man bent into the shape of a comma, or parenthesis, by years of janitoring was pushing a wide, silent broom down the dull gleam of the corridor.

"Have a nice holiday, Pete," Henry offered in passing. "Rest up if you can."

"You too, Mr. Veen, you too," Pete said with a low chuckle. Henry had tried to get him to call him "Henry," but he couldn't make the transition, somehow, so Mr. Veen he remained.

He pushed through the last set of swinging red doors

out into the cold, and there was the 53 bus, pulling up to the curb. He found a seat at the back, across from a young woman with beautiful eyes and lips the color of roses, and as he sat, he found it difficult not to stare, searching her calm face for some glint of response. It was funny, he thought, how in moments of fatigue and duress he sought consolation in women and their beauty; while he recognized his admiration as foolish, futile, he could not bring himself to stop staring and was almost relieved when she got out, stepping out into the cold.

At home, he was driven by that last bit of manic energy that had propelled him through the term and so, thinking vaguely of Pete and a life spent pushing brooms, he swept his own floor, did the dishes, straightened his desk, and then lay in a very hot tub, soaking out the term. He ate a makeshift dinner of bread and cheese and salad, read the paper, and then pondered the empty evening which, somewhat to his surprise, had opened up before him.

Although he had been alone, girlfriendless, for almost a year, his longest stretch of bacheloring since college, gone was that little jolt of excitement he experienced when he was first single—the pleasant glimmer of hope and expectation that came with the knowledge of freedom, guiltlessness, that he could do whatever he wanted and no one would know or care. But he soon realized that the price of freedom was solitude, and a kind of dull, persistent loneliness he had never felt before. And although he was exhausted, it was exhaustion less of the body than the spirit, depletion of the soul which, emptied out by teaching, now needed filling up. He had tried to call a few friends, but their phones had been answered only by machines, their canned spooky voices inviting him to leave a message. Instead he hung up, impulsively pulled on his coat and hat and went out into the cold. He made his way toward the bright lights of the avenue and then along it, past the coffee shops and stores toward "Sammy's," the bar where, once or twice a week, he stopped in for a drink.

At the corner a shred of newspaper leapt up and clapped against a chain-link fence, and in the same gust of wind his own hat tried to escape, but he caught it and stuffed it into his pocket. Inside the bar, it was warm, and he was consumed by the swirling fragrances of smoke and perfume and alcohol, all riding the pleasant undercurrents of laughter and conversation and music. Christmas lights hung above the bar, a cardboard Santa Claus reflected in the mirrored wall, and the place seemed gayer and fuller than usual. His usual place was taken, and so he moved around to the other, to the only vacant stool, next to a woman in a bright green dress. "Excuse me," he said. "Is anyone sitting here?"

She turned to him only long enough to say "You are, now," smile faintly, and turn back to her drink.

Most of the people in Sammy's were, unlike Henry, of brown, and not white, skin, a fact which, while it had initially made him wary and very self-conscious, he had long since gotten used to, once he realized that no one really cared. Indeed, he had come to prefer it there to places where he had once gone, frequented by people he vaguely knew from college who would run him through the familiar litany of questions, all designed to get him to reveal "how," and "what," he was "doing." And when he told them he taught social studies at a public high school in the city they would smile, say "that's interesting," and ask what he planned to do "after that." It was at moments like these that he realized he taught so he could spend his life around teenagers rather than adults.

Here at Sammy's he would usually sit alone gazing off into the warm, amber light as a familiar succession of sad, sweet songs played over and over on the jukebox and women drifted through the foggy field of his vision, lending form to the lilting cadences of pathos and desire. In the many times he had been there he had spoken only to the barmaid, a handsome young woman with skin the color of cocoa and hair in beaded braids, from whose blue-jeaned hip there always hung a cluster of keys, jangling and swaying in answer to her long, loose strides. She had responded to his pleasantries only with short, clipped sentences and Henry, not wanting to offend, or incur the wrath of her boyfriend, had stopped trying.

"Beer?" she now asked, leaning toward him.

"Thank you, please."

Around him sat the usual array of customers—the handsome man who always wore a suit and tie; the crowd gathered around the pinball machines; the couples, young and old, who sat at the tables in various postures of romance and repose. Along one wall a young woman sat alone, smoking and sipping a drink, and although he hadn't seen her before she looked vaguely familiar—her pretty round face, high cheekbones, the way her lips, when relaxed, fell into an amused, sardonic smile. Was she actually alone, or waiting for someone to arrive? He could never tell, in this bar, who was aligned with whom; even the woman who sat beside him, whose knees kept sliding out from under her dress, gave off the air of "takenness," and sure enough a burly man silently appeared at her side, his large arm wrapping itself around her narrow waist.

Henry was feeling reckless. His fatigue from the day, the week, the term, conspired with the beer and the paltry dinner he had eaten, to make him want to be with someone other than himself. Across the room the woman was still alone, and now and then, it seemed to him, she glanced over in his direction—or was this just hopefulness distended by desire? He had never been adept at "picking up" women, or even speaking with women he did not know, but he knew that if he kept sitting there thinking, he would defeat even the glimmer of possibility. So he took a gulp of beer, went to the men's room, washed his face, and on the way back veered off course and abruptly stopped at her table.

"Excuse me," he asked, leaning toward her. "Could I smoke one of your cigarettes?"

"What?" the woman asked, looking back at him, eyebrows raised.

"Could I smoke one of your cigarettes, please? I don't usually smoke; I just feel like it tonight."

"Oh, sure. Help yourself," she said, sliding the pack across the table. "Take two if you like. They're menthol, though."

"As long as it's tobacco," Henry said, and lightly laughed. He took a cigarette, she offered her lighter and a long, thin flame leapt up between them. For an instant he looked her full in the face—brown eyes, the wavering line of her lips, the way the ridge of her hair hovered over her eyes like the crest of a breaking wave.

"I've got plenty if you want another," she said. "Really. Take one."

"Oh, thanks anyway. One should be enough. I'll come back if I need it. Thanks." He nodded, strolled back across the room and sat down, and it was only then that he realized his palms were sweating, his heart racing, his face flushed with the moment of contact. Had he detected, in the trembling undercurrents of their brief exchange, a certain willingness to talk with him? But now that the initial inroad had been made, how could he pursue it, follow it up? In this brief exchange his fatigue had been displaced by desire, and by the time he finished the cigarette he had ordered another beer and finished half of that too.

When he looked back across the room she was no longer there, only a thin ribbon of smoke rising from the ashtray. His disappointment turned to irritation as someone tried to push in beside him, and then to mild, suppressed elation when he looked and saw that it was her.

"Do you mind if I get in here for a minute?" she said. "If I keep waiting it will be Christmas before I get a drink. I guess the waitress went on holiday early."

"Sure, help yourself," Henry said, trying to make room. He was immediately conscious of her perfume, her narrow waist, the smooth, brown skin of her neck on which a gold chain lay. And there was something about the way she stood and waited, the inclination of her head, the way she looked neither at him nor away from him but somewhere into space in between, so that their views were shared, that seemed an invitation to look at her and speak.

The woman at the bar appeared and took her order and Henry, not wanting to lose the chance, paused and said, "So how are you tonight?"

"Oh all right, I guess," she turned to face him. "A little tired, I guess, but that's normal for the end of the week. How about yourself?"

"I'm fine—tired, but I'll live. It's the end of the term, so I've had enough of teenagers for a while."

"You teach?"

"Yeah, at a high school in the city."

The woman nodded, and their brief exchange was interrupted by the arrival of her drink, for which Henry almost offered to pay, but then didn't. She stood beside him, beer in hand. "My feet are killing me. I've been on my feet all day, so I've got to sit down. Come join me if you want to, though." And Henry, shy but not foolish, accepted, picked up his beer and followed her to her table; her body, he thought, was like that of a fourteen-year-old girl.

"I'm Toni, by the way. With an 'i'."

"Henry. Pleased to meet you."

"I saw you sitting over there, and then you asked for a cigarette, so I thought you might want to join me. I get tired of sitting by myself sometime. But I don't think I've ever seen you in here before. Do you come in a lot?"

"Weekdays, mostly. I live around the corner, so I drop in for a beer sometimes. How about you?"

"Oh, I've been coming here for years. I know a lot of people, so I come and meet my girlfriends sometimes, and sometimes I just sit alone and have a drink or two. They always ask me why I sit alone, but I just like to, that's all. What's wrong with it? If you only sit with your friends you never meet anyone, so what's the point? It's all right if you're a man, but if you're a woman, forget it. They don't understand."

She was wearing a thin, purple sweater and a gold chain that hung down across the swale of her collarbone, and had a wide, pleasant face of subtle if not extravagant beauty—of the kind that Henry, several years before, would not have noticed. She was, he guessed, a few years older than he, and spoke with a faint, southern drawl; when he asked her where she was from she said "Alabama," slowly, in the cadence of a question.

"Yeah, I moved up here eight years ago with my husband. He was Puerto Rican—real light skinned—and when he went for the marriage license they tried to talk him out of it, because they thought he was white. They didn't want him marrying a black woman. When I heard that I told him that if we wanted any kind of life we better move north, so we did. We moved to New York, and when we split up my daughters and I came up here."

He was not surprised to hear she was a mother; she had about her a certain softness—a kind of fullness often absent in in women her age who had not yet had children.

"And how old are your daughters?"

"Thirteen and fourteen. Good girls, both of them. A little wild sometimes, like me, but good girls." Here she paused and looked at him, faintly smiling. "And I'm thirty-four, in case you're trying to figure it out. I married young."

He could not tell if her loquaciousness was due to the alcohol, or was simply the way she was, but he was happy just to sit and listen to her talk; he had always been adept at asking questions, deflecting conversations so he didn't have to do any of the answering himself. She told him of the people in the bar—the cops who always sat in the corner; the well-dressed man in the gray suit who, as it turned out, owned a chain of shoe stores; and Sammy himself, a plump, balding man who Henry had always thought was the cook.

"He always carries a gun," Toni told him. "You can see it on his back. That's why there's never any trouble in here. He's not afraid to use it."

"Do they mind white people here?" he asked.

"Uh, uh. Not here. Maybe down in Slatters, or some-place. Half these guys have white girlfriends anyway. I've had white boyfriends myself. The last one, a French guy, wanted to marry me, but uh, uh. I've been that route. I like him, but I told him, I need my independence. Once you've had it it's hard to go back."

"I know what you mean," Henry said and reached across the table and took one of her cigarettes. She lit it for him. "You look familiar to me, though," he said. "Maybe I've seen you in here sometime before?"

"Uh, uh," she said, shaking her head. "That's one thing you learn in a bank—names and faces. I would have remembered. I never forget a face, and if you remember their names they trust you, and that's the most important thing."

"You work in a bank?"

"In the city. I've been there for eight years. I'm a senior loan officer. I've never had any trouble with anyone. Some of the girls I work with are always looking over their shoulders, thinking they're being treated differently be-cause they're black. I take them aside right off and tell them—if they have a chip on their shoulder it's not going to work. I don't care what color you are—blue, black, white. If you do your work, fine; if not, you better quit, because someone else will."

The waitress finally appeared with two more beers, but when he offered to pay she refused, and then paid for them herself.

"That's all right. I just got paid, and besides, I don't like to owe anyone anything—they might want it back someday."

An amused, quizzical expression came onto her face, half-formed into a smile.

"You're married, right?" she said suddenly. "You live with your girlfriend?"

The question was so unexpected he laughed. "I haven't had a girlfriend in a year. Why?" he asked. "Do I look like it?" But she was already thinking of something else, staring up into the smoky air above his head.

The bar was now thinning out. The crooked clock on the wall read twenty till one, and the barmaids were beginning to get that anxious, unamused look they get around closing time. People pulled on their coats and drifted toward the door, stepped out, and then drifted back in, like a tide that could not quite decide to turn. Henry was happy where he was—drunk, but not overly so; queasy from smoking too many cigarettes; but relaxed and relieved to be sitting with a woman whom, vague sexual aspirations aside, he was simply happy to have met and spent the evening with. And he took it all as one of those rare gifts that came to him now and then in reward for his own perpetual, if tentative, efforts. He had already absolved himself from any fumbling attempts to get her phone number or address, preferring to leave things as they were and, if fate decreed, meet her there again.

"Are you tired?" she asked him. "You look kind of tired."

"Kind of, but not too. It's the end of the term—all those students and papers and crap to fill out. I'll be better tomorrow."

The lights above them were flicking on and off, and the woman with jangling keys was wiping the tables. Henry put on his coat and walked out with her into the cold. He only intended to see her to a cab, kiss her good night if the opportunity arose; but when one stopped, and she climbed in, she looked back at him with an expression both shy and surprised, and said, "Aren't you coming?" And the next thing he knew he was sitting beside her as the car drove off under a canopy of lights, her small, tepid hand folded into his. Her eyes fell shut, her head tipped against his shoulder, and Henry, given over to a sense of his renewed good fortune and with mild trepidation, looked out the window as they rumbled down the avenue, over a steel bridge that spanned an icy river, and then into a part of the city where he had never been. They passed onto an elevated subway and into a neighborhood of quiet streets and neat row houses, and it was then that he realized that they were not far from the school where, five days a week, forty weeks a year, four years so far, he taught. Why this should induce in him a sudden sensation of guilt, of wrongdoing—a lingering, Pavlovian throwback to his own school days—he did not know.

The cab pulled up in front of one of the houses, Toni stirred to consciousness and Henry paid with his last five dollars.

"Here we are," she said sleepily, slipped out into the cold and across a swath of frozen earth to the porch, back into warmth, and up a flight of creaking stairs.

"Watch yourself at the top, now," she said, and then pushed past him with the key into a warm, cozy room filled with books and plants and a fold-out couch. "That's where my daughter and her friend will sleep when they get back from their party. Come into the kitchen and I'll make you some tea."

He had forgotten, somehow, about her daughters. "Do they mind when you have friends over?" he asked, and she stopped in her tracks.

"I'm a grown woman," she said simply. "My daughters know that. Life doesn't stop just because you've had a couple of kids. I've got a life to live too. I'm only thirty-four years old."

Then the kettle began to hiss, and in the warm light of the kitchen her motions took on a kind of domestic reserve, some new and vulnerable aspect of her character revealed to him.

"Sugar? Milk?"

"Just milk please."

"Let's go in my room in case my daughter comes in. I don't feel like playing mother tonight." She turned out the light, and as she led him into her room it was with a pleasant sense of complicity—last experienced, he realized, when the roles were reversed and he was a teenager, tiptoeing around the backs of his girlfriends' sleeping parents.

A pale, whitish light fell upward from the street, and Henry sat in a small rocking chair by the edge of the bed, sipping his tea.

"I hope you don't think I do this all the time—'have friends over,' meet men in bars and bring them home. Sometimes you just want company, and you seemed like a nice person. Shy, maybe, a little shy. Some men think just because you've had kids you're looking for a husband, or a weekly paycheck. I've been married. I'm better off running my own life with my daughters. Having a man around just means more work."

"Some men," Henry said, in weak defence of his gender.

"Most men—at least the ones I've known, and that's more than one. Don't get me wrong. I love men. But between my daughters and my job I have enough work to do. I don't have time for looking after grownups."

"Don't worry. I'm not grown up yet."

"Yes you are. And you'll make someone a good husband someday. I can tell."

He took this as a compliment, and in lieu of answering leaned toward her, and in the instant before their lips touched saw them form something like a smile.

"Have you ever been with a black woman before?" she asked, shyly, but before he had a chance to answer she added, "It doesn't matter anyway. People are people."

Nor had he ever been with a married, or once-married woman, nor with someone who had children, and as they made love it was with the added sensation of this handful of taboos, half-sins, falling away in the face of other sensations: the smell of the clean and tangled sheets, sweat, perfume, shampoo; the cheerful scent of pine from a nearby miniature Christmas tree; the chiming of bells from a distant church; and, greater still, the simple fact of her body, bare and lovely and brown, warm on a cold night, next to his. And sometime later, deep into the folds of darkness, the ebb and flow of night, they fell asleep, then re-awoke, and the drama acted itself out again.

The next time he opened his eyes a pale, blue light pressed against the window; he could remember hearing some time in the night the sound of voices, laughter, and for a moment he had dreamed he was back in school, sleeping on his desk as the first of his students, followed by the principal, filed in for the day. It was a relief to know he was not in class, nor in his own apartment, but in an unfamiliar room, beside a woman he hardly knew.

Around him, the room was small but neat—shelves of books, a potted plant, the tiny Christmas tree he had smelled in the night. On the desk were piles of paper, a marmalade jar filled with pens, and, in a small glass frame, a photograph of two girls he took to be her daughters. The younger of the two looked vaguely, and then very, familiar, and it was with a shock of recognition that her face swam dreamily into focus, and found a place in his mind, memory, classroom—last row on the right, fourth period . . . a shy, quiet girl and mediocre student . . . Angelo, Maria . . . a slight girl with sleepy brown eyes, high cheekbones, and a lovely enigmatic smile inherited, he now knew, from her mother.

His initial reaction, like that experienced as a child when the rock he had just thrown veered off course at the last minute and crashed through a neighbor's window, gave way to other, more practical considerations: would she see him leave? Would word spread, from student to teacher to parent to administrator, and thereby terminate his career? But these and other questions swam through his mind at a safe distance and, despite their apparent gravity, failed to fill him with any great sense of urgency, or peril. He too, was a "grownup," and had done nothing that, given a second chance, he would not do again. It was oddly satisfying to realize he had, after all, been caught.

And even the suspicion of Maria, asleep in the adjacent room, only added to the circular mystery of it all, and lent a kind of credence, a validity to the paternal fondness he had always felt for her; and her presence there relieved him of trying to escape.

Instead, he lay back down, and gave himself over to the subtle satisfactions of the present: his clothes lay in an orderly heap beside the bed, the pipes hissed and clanged from some remote corner of the building, and outside plumes of steam rose from unfamiliar roofs as the blue-gray dawn grew bluer as the unseen sun slowly crept toward the horizon and the earth—a giant, spinning ball—slowly turned to meet it. Beside him Toni stirred, and then spoke—a string of softly murmered words whose meaning, though he tried to understand, he could not decipher. He looked over at her half-turned face, but her eyes were still closed and he lay back into the bed, closed his own, and began to drift toward something like sleep. What was she dreaming of? He would ask her later, when she woke.